'I would
share my **t**
be fair on

Meg knew what he was saying, that he was warning her that they had no future, yet she couldn't let it go without trying to make him see that he was wrong. 'Not all women would react like Briony did, Jack.' She took a quick breath. 'I wouldn't.'

He smiled, and there was tenderness in his eyes when he looked at her. 'I know that. However, it isn't a risk I intend to take ever again.'

What could she say when he had made up his mind? Nothing. She couldn't run from the pain she felt because it was locked inside her. Jack had said that he hadn't compared her to Briony, but he was still judging her by the other woman's actions!

Jennifer Taylor lives in the north-west of England with her husband Bill and children Mark and Vicky. She had been writing Mills & Boon® romances for some years, but when she discovered Medical Romances™, she was so captivated by these heart-warming stories that she set out to write them herself! When not writing or doing research for her latest book, Jennifer's hobbies include reading, travel, walking her dog and retail therapy (shopping!). Jennifer claims all that bending and stretching to reach the shelves is the best exercise possible. It definitely beats step aerobics…

Recent titles by the same author:

A VERY SPECIAL CHILD
A REAL FAMILY CHRISTMAS
FOR BEN'S SAKE
GREATER THAN RICHES

TOUCHED BY ANGELS

BY
JENNIFER TAYLOR

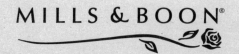
MILLS & BOON®

All the characters in this book have no existence outside the imagination of the author, and have no relation whatsoever to anyone bearing the same name or names. They are not even distantly inspired by any individual known or unknown to the author, and all the incidents are pure invention.

All Rights Reserved including the right of reproduction in whole or in part in any form. This edition is published by arrangement with Harlequin Enterprises II B.V. The text of this publication or any part thereof may not be reproduced or transmitted in any form or by any means, electronic or mechanical, including photocopying, recording, storage in an information retrieval system, or otherwise, without the written permission of the publisher.

This book is sold subject to the condition that it shall not, by way of trade or otherwise, be lent, resold, hired out or otherwise circulated without the prior consent of the publisher in any form of binding or cover other than that in which it is published and without a similar condition including this condition being imposed on the subsequent purchaser.

MILLS & BOON and MILLS & BOON with the Rose Device are registered trademarks of the publisher.

*First published in Great Britain 2001
Harlequin Mills & Boon Limited,
Eton House, 18-24 Paradise Road, Richmond, Surrey TW9 1SR*

© Jennifer Taylor 2001

ISBN 0 263 82652 X

*Set in Times Roman 10 on 11 pt.
03-0301-62069*

*Printed and bound in Spain
by Litografia Rosés, S.A., Barcelona*

CHAPTER ONE

'I KNOW it's short notice. Unfortunately, I only found out late last night that Yvonne wouldn't be fit enough to travel. However, I do realise that forty-eight hours isn't very much time to get ready, so if you feel that you can't make it, please, say so.'

'No, it's fine. Really.'

Meg Andrews had heard the hesitation in his voice and frowned. Even at her interview she'd sensed that Jack Trent had reservations about taking her on as a member of the team. Why? Her references were excellent and the experience she'd gained in the surgical wards of Dalverston General Hospital made her ideally suited to the work so why should he have appeared so...*reluctant* to accept her?

She shrugged off the faint feeling of unease, realising that it was pointless wasting time by worrying about it. There were more important things to think about, like where they would be going, for instance. She felt a little thrill of excitement course through her as it hit her that it was really going to happen at last.

As soon as she'd seen the advertisement in one of the nursing journals for experienced nurses to join a leading overseas aid agency, she'd known that was what she wanted to do. Oh, she loved her job and derived a great deal of satisfaction from it, but it was time for a different sort of challenge.

After the interview she'd sat back and waited to hear where she would be sent, but it seemed to have taken *months* before this phone call had come out of the blue that morning. Now she could hardly wait to hear all the details.

'So where exactly are we going?' Meg asked, unable to keep the excitement out of her voice. She caught a glimpse of herself in the mirror above the table where the phone was precariously balanced on top of a pile of textbooks, and grimaced when she saw the sparkle in her deep blue eyes.

She looked as excited as a sixteen-year-old being asked out on her first date rather than a mature, worldly woman of twenty-six being given details of her next professional assignment! She had to learn to contain her enthusiasm, but it was hard to maintain a calm front even though she sensed that Jack Trent would prefer that kind of approach…

'Sorry?' She suddenly realised that he'd said something, and hurried to get her thoughts back on track. It certainly wouldn't reassure him if she started daydreaming!

'Oncamba. I'm not surprised that you haven't heard of the place. Not many people have. It's a tiny state in south-eastern Africa, the merest pinprick on your map if you want to check out its location.'

Jack Trent's tone was level as his voice flowed down the telephone line—cool, concise, impersonal, like the man himself. Meg had a sudden mental image of him sitting in his immaculately tidy office, and was glad that video phones were still very much in the future. She could just imagine how those chiselled lips would curl disdainfully if he got a glimpse of the chaotic state of her flat, not to mention the way she was dressed that morning.

She bit back a chuckle as she glanced down at the misshapen black T-shirt—a cast-off from her brother—that she was wearing with jeans which had holes in both knees, and mentally compared it with what Jack Trent had been wearing the one and only time they'd met. He'd been resplendent in a severely cut black suit and pristine white shirt, a soberly patterned tie adding the finishing touch to the picture of professionalism he'd presented.

The fact that the clothes had suited his austerely handsome looks had been more by accident than design, Meg suspected. Jack Trent certainly hadn't struck her as a man who worried about his image, although admittedly he'd left a lasting impression on her. More than once in the months since that interview she'd found herself bringing him to mind, as she was doing now.

Meg cleared her throat, not sure why the realisation made her feel so uneasy. 'I see. I take it that background information on the state is rather limited in that case?'

'I'm afraid so. However, I can let you have what information I've managed to get hold of if you're interested?'

His tone implied that he couldn't imagine why she should be, and Meg bridled, mentally and physically. Of course she was interested! She was going to be working in the country, wasn't she?

'That would be a great help,' she replied, trying to keep the bite out of her voice. 'I would prefer not to go there without knowing anything at all about the people and their culture. It would make for a bad start to my mind.'

'You're quite right.' Jack Trent's tone had softened slightly and Meg bit her lip as she heard the mellifluous tones flowing down the line. She'd never realised before what a beautiful voice he had, although it was hardly surprising when up till now he'd only ever used that impersonal tone when speaking to her. It was an effort to concentrate as he continued.

'When you're working overseas you must always take account of local cultural practices. It's vital that we don't try to impose our views on the people we are treating as it can be extremely detrimental at the end of the day. The last thing we want to do is to end up alienating those we are trying to help.'

'I agree. I imagine it can be tempting to try to dictate how things should be done, but you must have to remind yourself constantly that what is acceptable in Britain might be totally unacceptable in another culture,' Meg replied firmly.

'Exactly. I'm pleased you understand that.'

Pleased *and* surprised? Meg frowned as she wondered if she'd imagined that edge in Jack Trent's voice. She didn't think so. He *had* been surprised by her correct assessment of the situation, and her heart sank as she found herself wondering if he was one of those doctors who didn't hold nurses in very high esteem.

She had worked with a few doctors like that in her time, men mainly, who believed that all a nurse was good for was to carry out their instructions. The idea that a nurse could be an intelligent, thinking professional in her own right was beyond them. However, if Jack Trent was of that ilk then she would make sure that he soon changed his ideas. She was nobody's handmaiden, neither was her only role in life to be at his beck and call!

'Oh, I assure you there won't be any problems in that area, Dr Trent,' she replied coolly. 'I'm well aware of the pitfalls of working in a developing country and intend to avoid them.'

'Really?' He sounded amused now, although Meg found herself unable to share the joke when she sensed it was at her expense.

'Yes, really,' she repeated firmly, feeling her temper move a notch up the scale, which in itself was a rare occurrence. Her good temper and patience were legendary in Dalverston General, her ability to rise above the trivial everyday annoyances which came with the job one of her strengths. It surprised her that Jack Trent had managed to get under her skin to such an extent.

She took a steadying breath, deliberately wiping all traces of emotion from her voice as she continued, 'I know that I don't have any hands-on experience of working overseas yet, but I've given this enough thought to feel fairly confident that I'll avoid the more obvious mistakes.'

'I'm sure you have given it some thought. However, you may find that any preconceived ideas you have will be totally at odds with what the reality of working in a developing country is like.' His tone was once more impersonal. 'I suggest that you wait until you get there before formulating your ideas, Ms Andrews. That way you won't be either disappointed or shocked by what you find.'

'Meaning what exactly, Dr Trent? That I don't understand that we shall be working under extreme conditions? That I'm not prepared for the ugliness of poverty and disease?' She gave a short laugh. 'Or that I have some romantic notion about going to Africa to play the ministering angel?'

'I meant exactly what I said, that it would be wiser to wait until you get there before deciding on the best approach to the job.'

There was no hint of annoyance in *his* voice, Meg noted, biting back the sharp retort that sprang to her lips. If he'd picked up on her irritation then he certainly hadn't taken any notice of it!

She took a deep breath before she spoke, realising that it would be foolish to promote a confrontation at this stage in their relationship. It certainly wouldn't help to improve Jack Trent's opinion of her, that was for sure.

'I shall bear that in mind, Dr Trent,' she replied coolly. 'I'm very much aware that I'm the newcomer to the team so I shall be happy to follow your advice.'

'Good. I'm glad to hear it. One of the things I must stress, Ms Andrews, is that we all work very closely when we are overseas. Teamwork is all important and there's no time to pander to anyone's ego.'

His tone was authoritative. Meg could picture him sitting behind his desk, his dark grey eyes full of that self-assurance which had been so evident at her interview as he'd set about making sure that she'd understood the ground rules. Where work was concerned, Jack Trent wasn't prepared to compromise but, then, she sensed that he wouldn't be prepared to do so in other areas of his life either...

Meg cut short that thought because there was absolutely no basis for thinking it. She knew nothing about the wretched man's personal life, neither did she want to! All she wanted was to be part of the team and be given the chance to put her skills to good use.

'I don't have any difficulty with that concept, Dr Trent. And I assure you that I'm well used to working as part of a team. However, to go back to what you were saying about Oncamba, is it possible that you could let me have whatever information is available before we leave?'

'Certainly. As time is at a premium I suggest that I fax the details to where you work. I take it that won't cause any problems?' he suggested levelly.

'Not at all. Everyone at Dalverston General has been extremely supportive about me joining the agency. The management and the board of trustees have assured me that my job isn't at risk and that I shall be granted leave of absence whenever I'm asked to go overseas,' Meg assured him. 'If you could fax the information through to Roger Hopkins, the hospital manager, he will make sure I get it. I think I gave you the phone number at my interview.'

'You did. I have it here.' There was a rustle of papers before Jack Trent said, 'So, if you're absolutely certain that you'll be ready in time to come, that's just about it. I take it that your jabs are up to date and that you have a current passport?'

'Of course,' Meg replied stiffly, wondering if he thought her a complete idiot. Naturally, she'd wasted no time in having all the necessary inoculations as soon as she'd learned that she'd been accepted by the agency...unless he was looking for a reason not to let her go with him even at this late stage?

The thought was more than a little disquieting but she chose to keep it to herself. What was the point in asking him when he would most probably deny it? Yet the thought that Jack Trent didn't really want her along on this trip wasn't the most auspicious of starts. She made up her mind that before it was over she would convince him that he'd been wrong to have doubts about her or her name wasn't Megan Louise Andrews!

'Right. Then all that needs to be sorted out is your visa, and I shall get onto that straight away now that I know you are definitely coming.'

Jack Trent's authoritative tones cut through her musings. Meg brought her thoughts back on track once more, afraid that she would miss some vital bit of information and thereby prove him right to have reservations about her suitability. She was going to have to be very much on her mettle from now on, it seemed.

'We fly out from Manchester airport on Thursday at six

p.m., which means you'll need to be there at least two hours beforehand to check in. Keep any personal luggage to an absolute minimum, though. Although we've been given free cargo space on the aircraft, we need every bit of it for our equipment.'

'We're taking everything with us?' she queried, trying to imagine the logistics of packing enough supplies for a trip like this.

'Not quite everything.' Jack Trent's tone had softened once more, and Meg's finely drawn brows rose when she heard the thread of excitement it held now. It seemed a contradiction in terms—Jack Trent displaying *excitement* about anything—so her interest was immediately piqued.

'What do you mean?' she asked, trying to imagine how he would look with a smile softening those chiselled lips. Her heart gave a small bump when she found it only too easy to imagine it, and she bit her lip, not sure why the picture that had formed in her mind was so unsettling. Jack Trent was handsome all right and she didn't dispute it, but she certainly wasn't *attracted* to him. The idea was ridiculous! However, it took several seconds before the beguiling image of his smiling face faded from her mind, and a couple more before she realised that he was speaking.

'I didn't think it would be ready on time but they pulled out all the stops. There's everything we need on board... consulting rooms, two operating theatres, even a small hospital bay if we need to keep any patients under observation, plus all the facilities to cater to our personal needs, of course.'

'On board... I'm sorry but I don't understand. On board *what* exactly?' Meg queried bemusedly.

He laughed deeply, the rich sound flowing down the line and making her heart flutter again. 'Sorry. I've lived with this night and day for almost a year now so I forget that other people aren't as clued up on this project as I am. We shall be using a converted steam train as our base while we are over there. It means that we shall be able to travel throughout the country and see far more patients than we could normally have done.'

'A steam train!' Meg couldn't keep the surprise out of her voice and she heard him laugh again.

'I know! Sounds incredible, doesn't it? Evidently, the train was shipped to Oncamba during the early part of the century and used for many years. However, it was left to rust until the new ruler discovered it when he came to power a couple of years ago. It's thanks to his determination to do something to help his people that this whole venture has got off the ground, in fact.'

Jack's voice was filled with admiration. 'He contacted the agency and asked for help, suggesting that if enough money could be raised then the engine would be the perfect means of getting around the country. Evidently, most of the roads had fallen into such a state of disrepair during the previous ruler's time that travelling about is a nightmare. We in turn contacted various charities and the outcome was enough money to have the train fitted out to our specifications.'

He paused and she wasn't deaf to the sudden flatness of his tone, such a marked contrast to the enthusiasm he'd shown just moments earlier. 'So, Ms Andrews, the *Oncamba Angel* will be not only your place of work but where you will eat, sleep and live for the next three months. While it will be better than working in a hut somewhere in the bush, it certainly won't be luxurious by western standards, so are you sure that you still want to come along?'

'That sounds almost as though you're expecting me to say no!'

Meg laughed but she could hear the edge in her voice and knew that Jack Trent must have heard it, too. Suddenly she didn't care what he thought, whether or not he would prefer her to take a coolly professional approach. Anger rippled through her as she held the receiver closer, wanting to be sure that he understood what she was saying.

'Yes, I want to come, Dr Trent, and, no, the thought of the lack of luxury doesn't bother me. You may be surprised to know that the only thing I'm interested in is doing this job to the very best of my ability. That's the reason I signed up with the agency, so that I could—in some small way—make a difference to the lives of people who desperately need help.'

She took a small breath, aware that she was trembling after her impassioned outburst. What Jack Trent thought of it she had no idea because it was a few moments before he spoke, and even then his tone gave away nothing about his feelings.

'In that case I shall look forward to seeing you on Thursday, Ms Andrews. Goodbye.'

He'd hung up before she could reply. Meg slowly replaced the receiver, wishing momentarily that she hadn't said what she had. But why not? She'd meant every word and she hoped that Dr Jack Trent had taken note of it. Whether he liked the idea or not, she would be at the airport on Thursday. She could hardly wait!

'Jack Trent! Not *the* Jack Trent I saw on television last night?'

Meg was on a late that day and had been getting changed to go on duty when her friend, Maggie Carr, arrived for work. Meg had just finished regaling Maggie with what had happened that morning and had to admit that she was surprised by what her friend had said.

'I don't know. I didn't watch television last night because I made a start on painting the kitchen,' she replied, frowning.

Maggie dragged her sweater over her head then shook back her hair. She and Meg were complete opposites in colouring. Maggie's olive skin and black hair hinted at her Mediterranean ancestry whereas Meg, with her long blonde hair, delicately fair complexion and deep blue eyes, was a typical English rose. Now Meg hid a smile as she saw her friend roll her eyes in a gesture reminiscent of her Italian mother. They were opposites in temperament as well as looks—because if she was noted for her even temper then Maggie was *renowned* for her fiery one!

'Typical! I might have known you'd miss it!' Maggie declared, stepping into a pair of blue cotton uniform pants. 'Anyway, it has to be the same guy—tall, good-looking, *extremely* good-looking, in fact, all sort of mean and moody, if you know what I mean?'

Meg raised her brows. 'Mean and moody? I don't know if that's how I would have described him, although, on second thoughts, maybe you're right.'

She pulled a blue cotton V-necked top over her head and smoothed it down her slim hips. 'He certainly didn't come across as all that welcoming when I spoke to him this morning. In fact, I got the distinct impression that Dr Trent had reservations about asking me to go on this trip.'

'Really?' Maggie was brushing her hair but she stopped to stare at Meg. 'Why do you say that? I mean, you've loads of experience thanks to working on the surgical wards and, from what I heard him saying last night, surgery is going to play a major part on this trip. Isn't he some sort of eye specialist?'

'That's right. Evidently, he works at St Augustine's as well as being a director of the aid agency. He's head of the oph- thalmology unit there. I believe he also spends a lot of his time lecturing, both here and abroad.'

'Busy man from the sound of it. Must make it difficult for him to find time for a private life.' Maggie twisted her hair into a knot and pinned it in place. 'Pity! He looked rather a dish to me, but you can't go by appearances, can you? You tell him where to get off, Meg, if he tries giving you a hard time. To my mind, he's lucky to have got you!'

Meg laughed as she slid her feet into a pair of comfortable rubber-soled clogs. 'Thanks for the vote of confidence! Can I have it in writing, please, just in case I need it in the next three months?'

'You aren't really worried that you might?' Maggie had been heading out of the staffroom door but she paused to look worriedly at her friend. Meg shrugged, feigning a nonchalance she wished she felt as she slipped past her friend and hurried towards the ward.

'Not really,' she fibbed, pushing open the swing doors and

smiling at Mrs Watkins who was in the first bed. 'As you say, I'll soon put Jack Trent in his place.'

'Attagirl! Good morning, Mrs Watkins. How are you today?' Maggie asked as they both automatically stopped beside the middle-aged woman's bed. Joan Watkins loved to chat, and all the staff made a point of stopping to have a word with her whenever they could spare the time. A widow whose grown-up children lived abroad, she had few visitors to break the monotony of her day.

She had been admitted as an emergency case, suffering from an obstruction of the colon. A temporary colostomy had been performed until she was well enough to have the blocked section removed, and all the staff had been impressed by her cheerfulness and positive attitude. Now she looked curiously at Meg.

'Morning, girls. Who were you talking about just now? Your boyfriend, was it, love? Is he giving you a hard time, then?'

Meg chuckled wryly. 'No, he isn't my boyfriend! He's someone I'm going to be working with for the next few months.' She quickly filled Joan in on the details of her trip, smiling when the woman shuddered.

'Oh, I don't think I'd fancy doing that! You never know what you'll catch, going to those sorts of places. What made you decide to apply for the job? Don't you enjoy working here?'

'I love it,' Meg replied sincerely. 'Both the work and the people I work with. I just feel that I want to try something different, use my skills to help people who so desperately need helping, and this seems the ideal way to go about it. I can work overseas for the aid agency, knowing that I still have my job here to come back to.'

'But how about your young man—what does he think about you going to a place like that? I bet he doesn't like the idea,' Joan persisted, obviously not convinced it was the right thing to do.

'I don't have a "young man". Or an old one for that

matter!' Meg laughed. 'I'm fancy-free at the moment and can do whatever I like. That's another reason why the time is right for me to take on a job like this. I don't have commitments at present but all that could change in a couple of years' time. I couldn't imagine leaving behind a husband and family while I flew off to the other side of the world to work.'

'Well, I expect you know what you're doing,' Joan conceded reluctantly. 'So when do you leave?'

'Thursday evening,' Meg replied, lifting Joan's chart off the end of her bed and glancing through it.

'And are they giving you a send-off, then?' Joan turned to Maggie. 'Surely you've got something planned to mark the occasion?'

'We hadn't but we soon will have! Great idea, Mrs Watkins. Why didn't I think of it?' Maggie shook her head as Meg opened her mouth. 'Don't waste your breath. I'm going to give you a send-off to remember!'

Meg groaned. 'Why do I have the feeling that I am going to regret this?'

She did regret it! On the way to the airport late Thursday afternoon, Meg couldn't think of anything she regretted more, in fact. She'd had only a few hours' sleep the night before and she felt completely exhausted. Between getting ready for the trip, finishing her decorating and working till eleven the previous night it had been a hectic couple of days.

Even when she'd finished work the previous night, that hadn't been the end of it. Maggie had rounded up a bunch of their friends and had dragged everyone off to a nightclub where she'd insisted that Meg have a glass of sparkling wine to toast her departure.

After a couple of hectic hours of dancing, Meg had pleaded tiredness as her excuse to leave, only everyone had suddenly decided that a curry would be the perfect ending to the night. Unfortunately, it seemed in imminent danger of making its reappearance so she was thankful when the taxi pulled up outside the departure terminal. Hopefully, a breath of fresh air would make her feel better...

'Where the hell have you been? I thought I told you to be here well before we were due to fly out?'

Maybe he hadn't *really* shouted but to Meg's sensitive ears it certainly felt as though he had. She turned slowly around and stared at Jack Trent, noting almost idly how angry he looked. Why? Because she'd turned up only five minutes before the alloted time? Or because she'd turned up at all?

'It is *five* minutes to four, Dr Trent,' she said as coolly as she could, because that last thought had stung. 'I wouldn't have thought there was any cause for concern just yet.'

'Wouldn't you indeed? Well, that's where you're wrong, Ms Andrews. As it happens, our flight has been brought forward and we're due to leave in less than an hour's time. So, if you wouldn't mind getting yourself inside, we can check in your luggage.'

He turned to walk inside the building but Meg stopped him by dint of a well-placed hand on his arm. Her fingers closed around the hard biceps and even though she was annoyed she couldn't help noticing just how very hard it was. That Jack Trent was in superb physical condition couldn't be disputed. However, his attitude left a lot to be desired!

He swung round to stare at her, his cold grey eyes dropping deliberately to where her hand was still attached to his arm. However, Meg refused to release him until she was good and ready. She certainly didn't intend to let him think she was afraid of him!

'What have you got against me, Dr Trent? It's obvious that you aren't one hundred per cent happy about me coming on this trip, and I think I deserve to know why, don't you?'

She was quite pleased with the tone of her voice which had sounded both firm and nicely controlled to her ears. However, if Jack Trent was impressed he gave little sign. His mouth curled into what could only be classed as a sneer as he took stock of her tired face.

'In that case, Ms Andrews, I may as well be honest and say

that I was against you being hired. If it had been left solely to me then you would never have been taken on by the agency in the first place.'

The bluntness of that statement cleared her head more effectively than anything else could have done. Meg stared at him in consternation. 'Why not? You saw my references and I know for a fact that they were excellent. I also have several years' experience on one of the most demanding wards in the hospital, so how can you say that?'

'Because it's the truth.' He gave a sharp downward thrust of his hand when she went to speak. It had the added effect of dislodging her hand. Meg let it fall to her side as she stared at him with troubled blue eyes that reflected her hurt and confusion.

He looked away and there was an odd note in his voice all of a sudden, almost as though he might have regretted speaking so bluntly. However, there was no softening to his attitude, Meg realised sickly when he continued.

'I don't believe that you will cope, Ms Andrews. That's it in a nutshell. It makes no difference how good your references are or how much experience you have—I just don't think that you will be able to handle this kind of work. It is a whole different ball game, working overseas, compared to where you've worked in the past.'

'I know that! I understand that we'll be working under less than ideal conditions if that's what you're concerned about.'

'I don't think anyone can truly understand what the conditions will be like until they've experienced them at first hand,' he stated coldly. 'Oh, I expect you've seen TV coverage of aid work but that's sanitised for the viewers' consumption. Actually, dealing with all the hardships and unpleasantness is an entirely different matter, believe me.'

'I do believe you! I know that I have a lot to learn but I'm willing to try. Why can't you at least give me the benefit of the doubt?'

'Because there isn't room on a trip like this for a passenger.

We need everyone to pull his or her weight from the outset,' he snapped back.

'I shall pull my weight!' she retorted, whipping up her anger because his words had hurt so much. Maybe it was the combination of the late duty, the decorating, the night out—not to mention the curry—that were all taking their toll, but she felt a lump come to her throat. However, she would walk over hot coals rather than let Jack Trent see that he'd upset her!

'What if I prove you wrong, prove that I can cope with this type of work?'

'Then I shall apologise, Ms Andrews. Now, if you're ready?' He picked up her bag, leaving Meg to follow him into the airport building.

She squared her shoulders, although she felt rather like a prisoner on her way to the gallows must have felt. Three months of working with a man who thought she wasn't up to the job and would be waiting his chance to take her to task didn't sound like a very appealing prospect! It was only the thought of the satisfaction it would give him if she backed out at this stage that firmed her resolve.

Forget the apology. Jack Trent was going to eat a large slice of humble pie at the end of this trip if she had anything to do with it!

CHAPTER TWO

THE journey seemed to take for ever so that Meg lost track of the hours they'd spent travelling. After they landed in Johannesburg they took an internal flight which just seemed to go on and on.

Meg knew that everyone was exhausted by the time they landed for the second time at a tiny airfield at the edge of the bush, but there was still another leg of the journey to undergo before they stopped for the night. Three small trucks were waiting to collect them and their equipment and ferry them to the Oncamban border, a good thirty miles away, where they would spend the night. Hopefully the next day they would complete their journey and board the train.

'Oh, how I hate this bit!'

Lesley Johnson, one of the two other nurses with whom Meg would be working, sighed as she plonked herself down on top of a packing case. A pleasant woman in her mid-forties, with bright red hair and a face full of freckles, she had gone out of her way to make Meg feel welcome. They'd sat in adjoining seats on the flight from Manchester and Lesley had kept up an undemanding conversation, telling Meg about previous trips she'd been on with the agency.

In fact, all the members of the team she had met so far had been extremely friendly. There were five of them in total plus another two who had flown on ahead and would meet them in Oncamba. Meg had just about managed to slot names to faces by now and was sure that she would enjoy working with such a lively bunch of professionals.

They seemed to have accepted her without hesitation, including her in the conversation when they'd stopped for a meal at Johannesburg airport. It was only Jack Trent who seemed intent on treating her as an outsider…

'Why this bit in particular?' She deliberately closed her mind to that thought, focusing instead on what Lesley had said. Right at that moment Jack Trent was busily supervising the loading of some of the more fragile equipment onto one of the lorries, and she doubted whether he was giving her any thought! She could see him out of the corner of her eye if she turned her head a fraction, his rangy figure clad in khaki chinos and shirt which blended with the landscape. He should have been virtually invisible in that outfit yet she had no difficulty picking him out. It was as though some sort of inner radar had immediately homed in on him.

'Because this last stage always seems to take ages!' Lesley declared. 'I mean, here we are just thirty miles away from our destination and we're all itching to get started, but if I know anything at all about these trips it's that there will be one delay after another, getting the equipment there. You take it from me, Meg, the flight from England is a doddle compared to hauling our stuff over these back roads!'

'Don't say that! Here I was thinking that it wouldn't be long before I'd be able to have a lovely long soak in the bath and wash off some of this grime!' Meg retorted ruefully, brushing the gritty sand off her dusty jeans. She looked up as a shadow fell over them and her heart skipped a beat as she found Jack Trent staring down at her. It was obvious that he must have overheard what she'd said because there was a mocking tilt to his lips as he treated her to a thin smile.

'I'm afraid long soaks in the bath are a luxury you'll have to learn to live without for the next few months, Ms Andrews. I did warn you, if you remember?'

'How could I forget, Dr Trent?' She returned his smile with an even thinner one but that didn't mean the comment hadn't stung. It wasn't pleasant to realise that he was only waiting his chance to take pot-shots at her. It was a relief when Lesley interrupted at that point because Meg wasn't sure what else he might have said.

'*Ms* Andrews? *Dr* Trent?' the older woman scoffed. 'Rather formal, isn't it, for a trip like this?' She sighed as she looked from one to the other. 'Don't tell me you two are going to stand on ceremony for the next three months. How about making that "Meg" and "Jack" and starting as you mean to go on?'

Meg shrugged although she was careful to avoid Lesley's eyes. Jack Trent *had* started as he meant to go on, that was the trouble! However, in the interests of team harmony it seemed wrong to make their differences common knowledge. 'Fine by me. I'd prefer it if you'd call me Meg, anyway.'

'Of course. And it goes without saying that you must call me Jack,' he concurred. He turned away before Meg could answer, raising his voice as he called to the rest of the party who were sprawled along the edges of the landing strip.

'We're just about ready now, folks. If you want to climb on board then we can make a start. The head driver assures me that it shouldn't take more than a couple of hours to reach the border, which means we should make it by five p.m. by my reckoning,' he announced.

'And if you believe that you'll believe anything!' declared Rory O'Donnell, the anaesthetist on the trip, and everyone laughed. Jack joined in as well and Meg felt her pulse miss a beat as she saw the austere lines of his face soften.

He looked so different when he laughed, she realised, even more handsome and attractive, just as she'd imagined he would look, in fact. Was it just that he had trouble unbending in front of her and found it easier to relax with people he liked and respected? She sensed that was so and her heart ached even though she didn't want it to.

She hurriedly got up when she realised that everyone was making their way to the trucks. Rory was giving Kate Gregory, another of the nurses, a boost up into the high cab amid a lot of teasing, his hands placed firmly on the woman's ample *derrière*. It was obvious that Kate was taking it all in good part as she shot a few pithy comments at her colleagues.

Meg smiled as she heard them laugh in response to whatever Kate had said. Obviously a good rapport was already building within the team and she felt her spirits lift. To heck with how Jack treated her—she intended to make the most of this trip and wouldn't let him spoil it for her!

'There's a few points I need to run through with you, Meg, so you may as well travel with me in the first truck.'

Jack didn't wait for her to reply as he strode towards the first of the three trucks which were lined up on the grass. Meg hesitated but there was no excuse she could think of to refuse his request, apart from one which was as unacceptable to her as it would be to him. To actually come out and tell Jack that she didn't want to travel with him because he seemed intent on making her feel miserable sounded too pathetic for words.

She followed him to the truck, colouring when he stepped back to let her climb into the cab first. The memory of how Rory had helped Kate was all the incentive she needed to make the ascent in double-quick time! She scrambled on board then quickly slid along the bench seat as Jack climbed up behind her and slammed the door.

He leant forward, his arm brushing the side of her breast as he pointed towards the driver. 'This is Moses. He's the head driver,' he explained, before settling back in his seat.

Meg smiled at the man beside her, trying her best to quell the sensations that were rippling through her. Although the touch of Jack's arm against her breast had been purely accidental, that didn't mean she wasn't very much aware of it. It was a relief to focus on the introductions rather than let her mind go spinning off at tangents, wondering why it should have had such an effect.

'Hello, Moses. It's nice to meet you. My name is Meg.'

The man gave her a wide smile, his white teeth flashing against his black skin. 'Pleased to meet you, Dr Meg.'

He started the engine, giving Meg no chance to correct him about her true status as the engine roared to life. The noise inside the truck was deafening for a few seconds before the gears engaged, and they set off with a shuddering lurch which pitched her sideways into Jack Trent.

Meg flushed as she quickly righted herself. 'Sorry.'

'Don't worry about it.' Jack placed a booted foot against the dashboard and braced himself as they jolted over another rut. His hand shot out and he grasped Meg's arm as she bounced on the seat. 'I know it isn't very ladylike, but try bracing your feet against the dashboard. It's the only way to keep yourself steady, I'm afraid.'

Meg did as he'd suggested and after a few moments found that he was right. It was easier to maintain her balance once she had something to brace herself against.

'Thanks,' she said with a grateful smile. 'It's a lot better like this.'

He shrugged dismissively, turning to stare out of the window as though, now that his duty was done, he intended to leave her to her own devices. Meg took a small breath, refusing to let slip the words she could feel welling up inside her. If he wanted to make it clear that he didn't care about her comfort then that was up to him. She certainly didn't intend to make a fuss if that was what he expected!

They travelled in silence for a couple of miles before Jack spoke again. Meg stiffened but, oddly, there was no hint of the expected hostility in his voice.

'Working out here will be quite a revelation for you, I imagine. I remember the first time I went overseas to work, not long after I qualified. I felt as though I should go straight back to med school because I was constantly being assailed with things I'd never dreamed I would have to deal with.'

He turned to look at her and his grey eyes were warm with the memory as he smiled. 'I used to lie in bed at night and pinch myself because I couldn't believe the things I'd seen and done throughout the day!'

'Then you've never regretted getting involved in aid work?' she queried, emboldened to ask by the fact that he seemed to have dropped the air of aloofness for once.

'Never.' He shook his head, pushing back a lock of hair which had blown over his forehead. Both of the truck's windows had been rolled down, although the breeze that flowed into the cab was almost as hot as the air inside it. Meg could see damp patches forming on the front of Jack's shirt where the cotton was sticking to his chest and knew that her own clothes were sticking to her as well.

When they lurched over another pothole and her arm brushed his, she could feel the heat of his skin burning into her and knew that the warmth of her skin had flowed into him. It was a strangely disturbing thought that their bodies' heat was mingling that way.

She cleared her throat, not wanting to think about it. Why should just the touch of this man's arm seem so very *intimate*? It didn't make sense. 'So you don't regret not devoting more time to your career, then?'

'You mean that if I didn't go on these aid trips then I could be at home, earning more money?' He gave a dry laugh. 'No, I don't regret it. Money isn't all that important to me, if you really want to know. I believe there are more important things in life than buying a bigger car or a more luxurious house, oddly enough!'

Meg frowned as she heard the acerbic note in his voice. Maybe he was just making sure that she understood he had higher ideals than that, yet there had seemed to be something more to that statement than had first appeared.

'I don't find it at all odd,' she replied quietly. 'I agree with you, in fact. Money isn't everything. It certainly doesn't buy true happiness. That comes from within yourself, from knowing that you are doing the things you want to do and that you are happy with the choices you've made.'

His brows rose steeply. 'A very altruistic attitude, Meg. I didn't realise that you felt that way.'

She shrugged, not sure that she liked the mocking note in his voice which seemed at odds with the searching look he gave her. 'You don't know anything about me, not about the sort of person I am, anyway. References and CVs aren't very much to go on when judging someone's character, are they?'

'Maybe not. But then I doubt if anyone relies solely on what's written on a piece of paper, even in a work situation.

I think most people rely on their instincts when they meet someone new.'

And his instincts had told him that she wasn't the sort of person he wanted to work with? It was on the tip of her tongue to ask him but she managed to contain the words. What was the point in asking him a question like that when she knew what the answer would be? It certainly wouldn't make her feel better to hear him state bluntly that he'd taken an immediate dislike to her.

She turned away before he saw the hurt in her eyes. She'd never been faced with this sort of situation before because she'd always got on well with the people she'd worked with. However, it was different with Jack Trent. Maybe it was foolish to be so sensitive but she couldn't help it.

'Is something wrong, Meg?'

She shook her head, hating the fact that he seemed to have sensed that she was upset. 'Of course not. I'm just hot, that's all.'

She took a tissue out of her pocket and mopped her forehead. Jack sighed as he settled back in the seat.

'It will get even hotter than this.'

'Then I shall just have to get used to it, won't I? I'm sure I'll survive, Dr Trent.'

'I'm sure you will.'

There was an odd note in his voice, which made her look at him. However, he wasn't looking at her but staring straight ahead, his gaze locked on the road as it wended its way through the bush. How, then, did she know instinctively that what had happened had upset him?

She had no idea yet she sensed it was true. Jack was upset because *she'd* been upset, and the knot of pain which had settled in the pit of her stomach eased a little. Maybe his attitude towards her wasn't set in stone after all, and she would be able to convince him that he'd been wrong to have doubts about her. The thought was enough to make her spirits lift.

He cleared his throat and she turned to look at him again, feeling her heart immediately sink when she saw that the aloof mask was firmly in place once more. What a fool she was to have imagined that he might have had a change of heart so soon!

'It will take a couple of days once we get under way to assess the kind of problems we're going to be dealing with. As you know, my main area of interest is eye disorders, but I shall be doing my share of general surgery, as well as dealing with whatever medical problems we encounter.'

'That was something I was going to ask you about,' Meg put in quietly, deliberately confining her thoughts to work because it seemed wiser. She was there to do a job, not to make friends and influence people, and she would be better off remembering that. 'I know a lot of these overseas aid trips specialise in various fields and I wasn't sure if that was what we would be doing.'

'Ideally it would be wonderful if we could specialise. Diseases of the eye, for instance, are a huge problem in a lot of developing countries. I would like nothing better than to spend the next three months devoting my time solely to that area. However, it just isn't practical,' he explained levelly. 'Oncamba has been cut off from the rest of the world for so long that the people have had no access to *any* sort of medical help for a great many years.'

'I see. So we are going to treat anyone and everyone we can—is that it?' Meg asked, frowning as she thought what a huge undertaking it was going to be.

'That's right. Oh, I shall still focus as much as I can on treating cases of trachoma and Guy, the other surgeon who has travelled on ahead to get things ready, has a keen interest in the early detection of cervical cancer. But, basically, you're right. We shall be seeing as many patients as we can fit into a day, no matter what type of problem they have.'

He frowned. 'It means that the workload is going to be very intensive so it certainly won't be the best introduction you could have had to this type of work.'

Meaning that he didn't think she would cope with the pressure? She almost laughed out loud as she realised just how foolish she'd been to imagine he might *care* about hurting her feelings when he lost no opportunity to try and undermine her confidence!

'Maybe not. But I'm sure I'll cope, Dr Trent, despite the fact that you're expecting me to fall flat on my face!'

She knew how unprofessional it was to speak to him like that and steeled herself for his reply. What she had never expected was that he would laugh.

'I'm sure that falling flat on your face is something you rarely do, Meg Andrews! I'm certainly not expecting or hoping it will happen either.'

His amusement vanished as abruptly as it had appeared. 'However, that doesn't mean that I've changed my mind. This isn't the sort of work for a woman like you.'

And what sort of a woman is that? Meg wanted to ask, only she didn't. She didn't need to because she already knew. Obviously, the sort of woman who didn't impress Jack Trent!

It wasn't a comforting thought when they would be working together for the next three months. Yet, if she was really honest, she would have been forced to admit that it wasn't just the fact that he held her in such low esteem professionally which hurt, but the fact that his opinion of her as a *person* obviously wasn't any better.

What a good job it was that she had no intention of being *that* honest!

It was getting dark by the time they reached the village where they would spend the night. Meg was as exhausted as everyone else as she scrambled stiffly down from the lorry. The last five miles of the journey had been a test of endurance and she was black and blue from being jolted around.

'Why on earth do we volunteer for these trips? I mean, I could be sitting in front of the telly right now with a cup of tea, watching *Coronation Street*. Must be mad, mustn't we?'

Lesley came to join her, rubbing her back as she tried to work the kinks out of it. Meg smiled sympathetically. 'I know what you mean. I thought my teeth were going to drop out on that last stretch!'

She grimaced when Lesley laughed then coloured as she caught the I-told-you-so expression on Jack's face as he strode past them to speak to Rory. Without stopping to think, she stuck out her tongue at his retreating back and heard Lesley stifle a snort of surprised laughter.

'Do I get the impression that you and our esteemed leader don't see eye to eye?'

Meg shrugged, wishing that she hadn't behaved so childishly. She certainly didn't want to cause problems within the team at this early stage. 'Sort of. Anyway, what happens now?'

Lesley took the hint and didn't pursue it, but Meg could tell that she was curious about what had gone wrong between her and Jack. What could she have said if Lesley had asked her what the problem was? Meg thought ruefully. That Jack didn't like her for some reason?

It was the truth and yet it seemed such a *feeble* explanation that she doubted anyone would believe it. Despite all the evidence to the contrary, Jack Trent didn't strike her as a man who took an unreasoning dislike to people.

That thought didn't help one bit—it simply served to make her feel even more perplexed. It was a relief when Jack announced that because of the lateness of the hour it might be better if they got straight to bed after they'd had something to eat.

It turned out that Moses lived in the village and his wife, Leah, had prepared a meal for them. Everyone sat round the fire while they ate the deliciously spicy stew the woman had made.

Meg hadn't realised just how hungry she was until then and had a second helping when Leah shyly offered it to her. She was a beautiful young woman with smooth, ebony skin, her hair intricately beaded and braided. She was obviously heavily pregnant, her distended belly clearly visible beneath the flowing, brightly coloured robe which covered her from neck to ankle. However, she still managed to move gracefully as she served their meal.

She smiled shyly when Meg thanked her. 'I am pleased that you enjoyed it, Doctor,' she said in her lilting voice, before she moved away to offer Rory a second helping, which was eagerly accepted.

'Why does she call us all "Doctor"?' Meg queried, spooning up another mouthful of the tasty concoction. 'I noticed that Moses did the same before, calling me *Dr* Meg.'

'Women come very low down in the pecking order in a lot of these African countries,' Rory explained, then glanced at Jack who was sitting beside him. 'Isn't that right?'

'Unfortunately, it is. We've found by trial and error that it's better if all the staff are awarded doctor status as it cuts down on a lot of problems, particularly with the male patients,' he explained, putting aside his empty plate. 'They accept treatment from a female doctor far more readily than they would accept it from a nurse. On trips like this, our nurses are more nurse *practitioners* than anything else, responsible both for diagnosing and prescribing treatment in many cases.'

'And you have no problem with that?' Meg asked before she could think better of it. She shrugged when everyone looked at her, glad that the heat of the fire could be blamed for her suddenly heightened colour.

'A lot of doctors don't hold nurses in very high esteem,' she muttered uncomfortably.

'Not a sin that I'm guilty of, believe me. And especially not on an undertaking like this. Everyone's input is equally important to the success of the operation, which is why everyone is expected to pull his or her weight.'

Was she the only one to feel the sting in the tail of that statement? Meg glanced round the assembled group but not one of them looked as though they suspected Jack had meant that as a warning. It was hardly surprising when it had been aimed at her, though, was it? Hadn't he said much the same thing earlier, that she was expected to pull her weight? Maybe he was taking the opportunity to remind her?

Suddenly, Meg knew that she'd had enough for one day. She was sick and tired of being in the dog house when she hadn't done anything to deserve it! She scrambled to her feet, avoiding Jack's eyes as she smiled at the rest of the team.

'I don't know about you lot, but I'm worn out. I think I'll call it a night if nobody minds.'

'Well, I don't for starters.' Kate got up as well, groaning as she arched her aching back. She shot a wry look at Jack. 'Yvonne was right to cry off at the last minute if you ask me. I bet she *knew* you were going to have us bouncing around over miles and miles of dirt tracks!'

Jack laughed deeply as he rose to his feet. In the flickering glow from the fire, his face looked almost saturnine until he smiled, and then there was such a transformation that Meg had to look away, because she didn't like the way her heart had started to bounce up and down.

It was only a smile, for heaven's sake! she told herself sternly. And it hadn't even been directed at her. Yet her foolish heart was playing leap-frog with her ribs.

'You could be right about that. I should have told her that we'd be travelling by limo and then she might have felt well enough to come along.' He sighed as he looked at the others. 'I'm sure we're all going to miss her.'

Especially when he'd been saddled with a replacement he didn't want!

Meg turned away, afraid that the hurt she felt would show on her face. Was he deliberately trying to be cruel? she wondered sickly as she hurried towards the hut she'd been allocated to sleep in.

'Meg, wait a moment!'

She paused when she heard Jack calling her name, although she didn't turn round because she wasn't sure that she had her emotions in check sufficiently to face him. She kept her back towards him, staring at the inky blackness of the trees that surrounded the village, yet she knew to the second when he stopped behind her.

That inner radar again, working overtime, she thought with

a surge of black humour. Maybe she should use it as an early warning system for whenever he was in the vicinity. She certainly could do with avoiding him from the look of it!

'I didn't mean that as it sounded.' He got straight to the point without any preamble, surprising her enough so that she half turned. She saw the regret in his grey eyes and somehow that undid all her good work, setting free her carefully shored-up emotions. It had been a long, tiring day and Jack's intransigent attitude hadn't helped one bit!

She felt her lower lip quiver before she could stop it and quickly turned away, hating herself for letting him see that he had the power to upset her.

'Oh, hell!' He reached out, as though he was going to touch her, then let his hand fall to his side without actually making contact. 'Look, Meg, I wasn't trying to make you feel that I wanted Yvonne here instead of you,' he ground out, as though the words had cost him an awful lot of effort.

Maybe they had, Meg thought with unaccustomed cynicism. It certainly couldn't have been easy for Jack to *lie* for the sake of harmony within the team!

'Don't worry about it,' she said with an insouciance which cost her even more. 'I certainly shan't!'

He didn't actually grind his teeth but the effect was much the same. Her blue eyes widened when she saw myriad emotions cross his face at that moment. It was a measure of his strength of mind that he managed to control himself, but she was shaking in her boots.

Why in the name of all that was holy did she *know* that he'd been tempted...*sorely* tempted...to kiss her? She had no idea but the thought was enough to make her head spin.

'I apologise, anyway. Goodnight.'

He strode away, leaving her standing there, staring after him. Meg took a tiny breath and let it trickle into her lungs. A bigger one might have helped but she didn't seem capable of that. Breathing was an effort, thinking even more of one, but feeling...well, feeling was easy-peasy!

She shivered as a hot trickle worked its way *up* her spine, shuddered as a cold one flowed the other way. Hot and cold chills were suddenly racing through her body however they chose and she couldn't stop them!

She closed her eyes and tried to subdue the little devils but that was a mistake of gigantic proportions. Jack's face suddenly filled her mind—lean cheeks, moody grey eyes, enticingly *kissable* lips…

'Oh!' Her eyes shot open before her wayward mind could go any further. Stills she could just about deal with, but if that picture had become animated and moved to the next frame— a close-up of the kiss Jack had so very *nearly* bestowed on her…

She groaned then clapped a hand over her mouth in case anyone heard her. She had to get a grip! So what if Jack *had* been tempted to kiss her just now? It didn't mean that she would have let him or responded. It took two to tango, as her mother was so fond of saying, only that didn't sound nearly as reassuring as it should have done. While she had absolutely no desire to tango with Jack…

She cut the rest of that thought dead!

Meg wasn't sure what had woken her. She was so tired that it was a wonder anything had. Yet suddenly she found herself wide awake and staring round at the darkness. Lesley was snoring softly in the adjoining campbed so obviously whatever had woken Meg hadn't disturbed her.

For a moment she debated rolling over and going back to sleep, but the nagging feeling that something was wrong wouldn't go away. Pushing back the mosquito net, she took her shoes from the end of the bed and shook them to dislodge any creepy-crawly visitors before slipping them on her feet.

Leah had left them a candle to light the hut with while they'd got undressed but they'd blown it out and now there was only the pale shimmer from a sickle moon to see by as Meg made her way to the door. She peered out across the clearing in the centre of the village and felt her skin prickle with alarm when she saw shadowy figures moving about in front of one of the huts. What was going on? Who was out there? And, more importantly, should she go and find out?

Meg hesitated but the feeling that something was wrong wouldn't go away. Her legs felt like lead as she stepped from the relative safety of the hut and began to cross the clearing. It was a relief when she spotted Moses among the crowd of people gathered by the hut.

'Is something wrong?' she asked, going straight over to speak to him.

He turned to her and his face looked grey and drawn in the moonlight. 'It is Leah, Dr Meg. The baby is coming but there is something wrong and he cannot be born.'

He gave an expressive shrug which said more than any words could have done. Meg felt her heart sink as she wondered what the problem might be. There were so many things that could go wrong during a birth, although thankfully most could be dealt with in the safety of a hospital. However, this was the middle of the African bush and she had no idea what she was letting herself in for as Moses eagerly accepted her offer of help. At that moment, it seemed a very long time since she'd done her stint on the maternity unit.

The hut was lit by candles, and as Meg went inside she could see several women gathered around the low pallet that Leah was lying on. It was obvious that they were the local midwives and she was conscious that she might offend them if she offered her help. However, they made no objection when she knelt beside Leah, simply moved aside to make room for her. She had a feeling that they believed they'd done all they could and her heart sank even further at that thought, although she tried not to show any trace of concern.

'Hello, Leah. It's Dr Meg,' she said softly, noting the lines of pain that bracketed the girl's mouth. 'Can I just check how your baby is doing?'

Leah nodded mutely. She was obviously too exhausted to speak. She arched upwards as another contraction began, a keening wail coming from her as the pain tore through her body. Meg was shocked by how strong her contractions were because there had been no sign that she'd been in labour when she'd served their meal a few hours earlier.

She placed her hand on the young woman's abdomen and gently palpated it, feeling the hard form of the baby beneath her palm. She couldn't be certain but she suspected that it was lying in the breech position and that was what was causing the problem. Turning the baby was beyond her because she simply didn't have that kind of expertise. However, it was obvious that something had to be done—and quickly—otherwise both mother and child could die.

She patted Leah's hand, trying to sound a lot more confident than she actually felt. 'Don't worry, Leah. I'll go and get another of the doctors and we'll help you deliver your baby. All right?'

She wasn't sure that the girl had even heard her as Leah stared at her with pain-glazed eyes. Meg hurried from the hut and ran across the clearing. Whether it was professional courtesy or pure instinct which made her go straight to Jack's hut, she wasn't sure, but she didn't stop to debate it as she ducked under the low lintel. Leah needed help and, in her view, Jack was the best qualified to give it.

'Jack, wake up!' Pushing aside the mosquito netting, she put her hand on his bare shoulder, ignoring the frisson which shot up her arm as she felt the heat of his skin. He was naked from the waist up, a thin white sheet covering the lower half of his body and outlining the narrowness of his hips and muscular power of his long legs.

Meg quickly averted her eyes and focused on the task of waking him rather than letting her mind go wandering off. All right, so Jack *was* superbly fit but now certainly wasn't the time to be thinking about it. She tightened her grip on his shoulder and shook him. 'Wake up, Jack!'

He came to in a rush, grabbing hold of her and rolling over in one swift movement. Before she knew what was happening, Meg found herself flat on her back with Jack looming over her.

'What the devil…?' For a moment he looked as stunned as

she felt before a slow smile spread across his face. Meg felt her heart go into overdrive because it wasn't a nice sort of smile by any means. Wolfish. Mocking. Sexy, certainly, but definitely not *nice*!

'Well, well. What have we here? Don't tell me that you're hoping to improve my opinion of you *that* way, Ms Andrews?'

CHAPTER THREE

'I...YOU... Let me go!'

Meg rolled to her feet as soon as Jack had released her. Pushing back her tumbled hair, she glared at him. 'What the hell do you think you're doing?'

He lay back against the pillow, a thin smile curving his mouth. 'I think I got my question in first, don't you?'

Meg felt a rush of colour wash up her face and was glad that it was so dark that he couldn't possibly have seen it. Did he honestly believe that she would have tried to influence him by offering to *sleep* with him?

The thought sent another surge of heat through her veins which she decided owed itself to anger. It had *nothing* to do with the remembered feel of his powerful body as it had pressed hers into the mattress, no connection *whatsoever* to the fact that just for a moment she'd found herself actually enjoying the contact. She was angry because never in her life had she been so...so insulted!

'If you imagine that I shall dignify that question with an answer then think again!' she snapped back.

'In that case, you'll understand if I don't answer your question, won't you? Anyway, I suppose there must have been a reason why you saw fit to wake me even if it isn't the one that sprang to mind. Is something wrong?'

She very nearly turned round and marched right out of the hut. She had sensed all along that Jack had a low opinion of her but she hadn't realised before just how low it was. It was only the thought of Leah which helped curb her temper and remember what she was doing there in the first place.

'Leah's in labour but there seems to be a problem,' she explained through gritted teeth. 'I might be wrong but I think

37

the baby could be breech. Can you come and take a look at her?'

'Of course.' He was out of bed before she could blink, stepping into his trousers and dragging on his shirt as he headed for the door. Meg hurried after him as he strode across the clearing, answering the questions he shot at her to the best of her ability. She felt a trifle stunned by the speed of the transformation as he'd switched back to total professionalism in the blink of an eye. Obviously, work came first on Jack's list of priorities and everything else came a very poor second. Why didn't that surprise her?

Jack went straight to the bed. Kneeling down, he smiled reassuringly at the young woman. 'Dr Meg tells me that you're having trouble, Leah—may I see?'

'Yes…' Leah's voice was weak with exhaustion and Meg found it difficult to hide her concern as she knelt beside the bed and took her pulse. It was so thready and faint that Meg's heart plummeted because she knew Leah wouldn't survive if something wasn't done soon to help her.

Jack looked up and his eyes reflected her concern as he looked at her across the bed. 'The baby is lying horizontally rather than breech from the feel of it. There's no chance of it being delivered normally because its arm and shoulder appear to be jammed in her pelvis.'

Meg swallowed as she realised the implications. 'She needs a Caesarean section, you mean?'

Jack nodded. 'Yes. There isn't any other option open to us at this stage. The only way to get that baby out is by doing a section otherwise we're going to lose both of them.' He glanced at the young woman and for a moment his face contorted with pain. 'It might be too late even now but we have to try.'

Meg didn't question his judgement because she knew he was right. If they didn't operate immediately then both Leah and her baby would die. She stood up and there was a new determination in her eyes when she looked at Jack. Even if there was only a slim chance that they could save them then they had to try.

'What do you want me to do first?'

Jack stood up as well and she felt her pulse leap as he smiled at her because for the first time ever there was a trace of admiration on his face. 'Reckon we can do it, then, Meg?' he asked quietly, his voice sounding very deep.

She squared her shoulders, striving for a calm she wished she felt, but it was hard to achieve that state when it felt as though dozens of butterflies were fluttering around inside her stomach. To see Jack look at her that way was everything she could have wished for, even though she wasn't sure why it should have mattered so much.

'Yes. If anyone can help Leah, I know you can,' she said quietly, knowing in her heart that it was true.

He inclined his head in brief acknowledgement but that didn't mean she missed the flare of some other emotion in the depths of his eyes…

She turned away before her mind could start racing along paths there simply wasn't time to follow right then. She focused strictly on what Jack was saying as he rattled out a list of instructions. Fortunately, they had all the supplies they could possibly need close to hand, although the thought of performing the operation under such conditions was daunting.

In the end, Meg decided that it would be better not to think about it and just get on with the job. If they didn't operate, Leah and the baby would die. There simply wasn't a choice so she had to accept the problems and deal with them.

'Do you want me to fetch Lesley or Kate?' she offered once she was sure she knew exactly what he wanted doing.

He shook his head. 'No, there's no need to disturb them just yet. I'll get Moses to wake them if I think it's necessary, but I'm sure you and I can cope, Meg. However, I will wake Rory. We'll need him to give the anaesthetic.'

Meg nodded her agreement before she hurried away to collect what was needed, but she couldn't deny that her heart had lifted when she'd heard Jack say that. Maybe he was beginning to trust her after all? Odd how much comfort she derived from that thought.

Afterwards, when Meg looked back on that night, she found it hard to believe that she hadn't dreamt it. There had been a surreal quality to the whole event which made it hard to believe it had actually happened.

At Jack's insistence, more candles and an old paraffin lamp had been brought into the hut to supplement the inadequate lighting, but conditions for performing the operation had still been far from ideal. It had been quite a struggle too to source basic supplies and equipment from the packing cases in the trucks.

They'd had to leave Leah on her bed for starters, as there had been no other suitable surface to use. Meg had covered the straw mattress with several sterile sheets, then had brought in a packing case to lay their implements on, draping that as well with a sterile cover. It had seemed very inadequate protection against infection but it had been the best she could do in the circumstances.

Jack had scrubbed up, then let her help him into a gown, holding out his hands so that she'd been able to snap the thin surgical gloves onto his hands.

'We need to double-glove for this,' he advised her softly. 'It would be foolish to take any risks.'

Meg nodded as she went to fetch a second pair large enough to fit him. Aids was endemic in many African countries so she knew he was right to take extra precautions. She followed his lead and put on a second pair of gloves herself, before going to assist him.

Rory looked up and grinned when they joined him by the bed. 'Typical, isn't it? You think you're going to have a nice peaceful start to things and suddenly find yourself thrown in at the deep end!'

Jack's brows rose. 'How many of these trips have you been on now? And when has anything ever gone the way we'd planned it? I think I'd worry more if it did!'

Both men laughed ruefully. It was obvious to Meg that they had a great deal of respect for each other and she found herself thinking how wonderful it must be to be an accepted part of the team. She shot a look at Jack and smiled to herself. Still, maybe things weren't quite so black as they'd appeared a few hours earlier if he was prepared to let her help him?

'Right, let's make a start if you're happy with everything, Rory? We can't afford to waste any time.'

Jack glanced at the younger man who nodded. Leah had been given an epidural anaesthetic as the risks to both mother and child were far less than if she'd been given a general anaesthetic in her weakened state. She hadn't made a murmur when Rory had injected local anaesthetic into the epidural space surrounding her spinal cord. It was obvious to Meg that Leah was completely worn out by the ferocity of her labour and she knew that the sooner it was over the better. As to whether they would be able to save both mother and child, that was something they would have to wait and see, but she murmured a fervent prayer that everything would go in their favour from here on.

'Scalpel.' Jack's face was set with concentration as she slapped the razor-sharp knife into his gloved palm. He swiftly and deftly made a horizontal incision in Leah's abdomen just above her pubic bone. Meg stood beside him, watching intently as he carefully slit through the lower part of the uterus. She could see the baby now and held her breath as Jack lifted it free and handed it to her, working swiftly as he tied and cut the cord.

'Right, it's up to you now, Meg,' he told her tersely, turning his attention back to the young woman.

Meg didn't say anything because there wasn't any time to waste. It was a baby boy and she could see at once that he was in some distress. Carrying him swiftly away from the makeshift operating table, she sank onto a chair and laid him across her knees then used a thin piece of sterile tubing to suction the mucus out of his mouth. He hadn't cried as yet and her heart was racing as she tipped him head down so that any fluid he might have swallowed would drain from his lungs.

'Come on, poppet,' she muttered, willing the tiny scrap to take his first breath. 'Come on, you can do it!'

She tapped the soles of his feet, mentally running through everything she knew about childbirth. Since she'd learned that she'd been accepted by the agency, she'd spent hours poring over her textbooks, brushing up on skills which had become a bit rusty through lack of use. However, all the reading in the world couldn't compensate for hands-on experience and she prayed that she would be able to help the child. She would never forgive herself if he died!

Laying the baby across her knees again, she placed her mouth over his nose and mouth and gently breathed into his lungs, willing him to respond. There was no sound in the hut apart from the measured rhythm of her breathing as time after time she inflated the infant's lungs. When Jack appeared beside her Meg didn't look up because she couldn't afford to let her concentration lapse. This child was relying on her and she *had* to help him!

'You've done all you can, Meg.'

Jack's tone was low but she heard the regret it held and tears welled into her eyes as she realised what he meant. The thought that the baby had died before he'd even had the chance to live was too much to bear.

She breathed into the tiny rosebud mouth once more, refusing to accept that there was nothing she could do for him…

The tiny body suddenly twitched, the baby's arms and legs shooting out as he began to squirm. Meg's face broke into a radiant smile as he let out a weak little wail when she raised her head. Within seconds he was crying in earnest, the sound of his irate screams ringing around the hut.

'We did it!' she declared, uncaring that tears were streaming down her face as she looked up at Jack. 'He's going to be all right!'

'*You* did it, Meg, you mean. You and your determination!' He uttered a joyful laugh while the baby continued to roar his disapproval of the new world he'd found himself in. 'By heaven, but he's got a fine pair of lungs from the sound of it!'

Meg stood up, aware that she was trembling as she quickly wrapped the baby in a towel. He needed bathing and checking over but all that could wait a few minutes longer. Right at that moment he needed his mother more than anything else.

Her heart contracted as she realised that she had no idea how Leah had fared. It took every scrap of courage she could dredge up to turn to Jack and ask him because she was so afraid what the answer might be. 'Is…is Leah all right?'

He squeezed her shoulder and his grey eyes told her that he understood exactly how she felt. 'She's fine, or she will be once she sees that young man.'

Meg could barely contain her joy. She smiled at him and saw his eyes darken. Her breath seemed to catch tightly in her chest when she saw the glitter of something hot and wild appear in their depths before he abruptly turned away and went to speak to Rory, who was clearing up.

Meg hugged the screaming baby to her as she hurried to the bed and knelt down. It was neither the time nor the place to think about what she'd seen in Jack's eyes just now, to wonder why he'd looked at her with such hunger. If Jack didn't like her then why should he *want* her? It didn't make sense.

'My baby!' Leah's exhausted face lit up as soon as she saw her child. She held out her arms, smiling in delight when Meg gently laid the baby in them.

'It's a boy, Leah, a lovely little boy.' Deliberately, Meg forced the unsettling thoughts to the back of her mind, although it wasn't possible to erase them completely. Jack was attracted to her? Was it possible? Everything that had happened so far pointed to the fact that she must have made a mistake and yet she couldn't quite convince herself of that.

'A boy?' Leah's eyes were full of wonder as she unwrapped the towel and stared at her baby son. She looked up and there were tears streaming down her cheeks as she tried to smile at Meg. 'Thank you…thank you!'

It was hard to contain her own emotions in the face of the young mother's joy. In the end, Meg gave up trying. Tears poured down her face, too, as she squeezed Leah's hand. 'I'm so pleased for you, Leah!'

She gave a shaky laugh as she got up and dried her face on the hem of her gown. 'What a pair we are! Now, I'm sure that Moses must be dying to see his beautiful new son so I'll go and fetch him.'

Leah smiled as she undid her robe and placed the baby to her breast, where he immediately began to suckle. 'My husband will be very proud. Every man wants a son,' she said simply.

Meg turned away, knowing that the picture of the young mother and her child would stay with her for a long time to come. Rory was still busily clearing up and he patted her on the shoulder as she passed him.

'Well done, kiddo. A first-rate job, I'd say. Welcome to the team!'

Meg smiled back, appreciating the genuine warmth of the comment. 'Thanks.'

She left him to finish what he was doing and hurried outside. She paused when she saw Jack talking to a smiling Moses. It was obvious that he'd already given the proud father the good news so she turned to go back inside then stopped when Jack called out to her. She went to join the two men, smiling when Moses grabbed her hand and began pumping it up and down.

'Dr Jack explained that it was you who saved my son. Thank you, Dr Meg. Thank you!'

'It was my pleasure,' she replied sincerely. He gave her hand another enthusiastic shake then hurried into the hut, closely followed by several members of his family who had been waiting outside.

Meg grimaced when she found Jack watching her as she

rubbed her throbbing fingers. 'I'm glad it wasn't twins! I think I may have a couple of crushed bones from the feel of it.'

He laughed deeply, his teeth gleaming whitely in the darkness. 'He was certainly pleased and no wonder. You did a great job just now, Meg.'

He moved away from the hut and it seemed the most natural thing in the world to go with him. They crossed the clearing, bypassing the huts on the other side and only stopping when they reached the trees which surrounded the village. The night was very dark, the moon just a slim silver curl in the velvety sky, a myriad stars scattered like diamonds across it.

Meg drew in a deep breath, tasting the unfamiliar scents carried on the night air. She was tired from all the travelling and lack of sleep yet she felt so elated that she wanted to shout for joy. As first days went it could have been worse…a lot worse, in fact, bearing in mind what had happened earlier. Had Jack's attitude towards her improved?

It was too tempting to resist finding out so that she didn't stop to think about the wisdom of asking the question. 'So, do you believe now that I can cope with this job?'

He turned to look at her, although his face was shadowed by the overhang of the branches. 'I think that you handled what happened just now extremely well.'

'But?' Meg laughed but there was scant amusement in the sound. She might not be able to see him clearly but she didn't need to because she'd heard the reservation in his voice. She turned to face him, unaware of how defensive she looked as she stood there in the watery moonlight.

'There was a definite "but" tagged onto that sentence, Jack, wasn't there?'

'Yes, I expect there was.'

He shrugged, his broad shoulders rising and falling beneath his half-buttoned shirt. He looked tired, too, Meg noticed when he stepped out from the shadows. There were deep lines bracketing his mouth and a lack of animation about his expression which made him look older than the thirty-six years she knew him to be. However, tired or not, he obviously didn't intend to opt for the easy route. Where work was concerned, Jack would never compromise!

'It's fair to say that you handled yourself well tonight, Meg. However, that doesn't change anything. I still don't believe that this is the job for you,' he stated flatly.

'Because I might not pull my weight? Or because I might not be able to cope with the conditions we're going to be working under?' She laughed harshly. 'Come on, Jack! You've just admitted that I acquitted myself well tonight so you'll have to do better than that!'

'Yes, you did do well tonight and I'm happy to admit it. However, one night's work isn't proof that you'll be able to keep up once the pressure is on.' His tone was unyielding. 'It's far more difficult trying to deal with the daily grind involved in this type of work, as you'll soon discover for yourself.'

'I'm sure you're right but I know that I shall cope no matter how hard it is. So it seems that we're at a bit of an impasse, doesn't it?'

Meg stared back at him, wishing there was a way to make him see that he was mistaken about her. It wasn't going to be easy, though, if Jack had made up his mind.

'It seems like it.' He shrugged again but she saw the irritation in his eyes. Obviously he wasn't used to people questioning his judgement, Meg thought. Well, tough! He wasn't going to have things all his own way if she had anything to do with it!

'Anyway, it's late and it's time you got some sleep. We'll be leaving early in the morning as we still have some distance to travel before we reach our destination.'

He turned to leave but Meg stopped him. Maybe it was pointless trying to discuss this problem he had with her being along on the trip, but that didn't mean she wasn't going to do the job to the very best of her ability. Was that what Jack was hoping? she wondered suddenly, that she would become so dispirited that she would make a mistake and prove him right?

She didn't really believe that yet she refused to dismiss the idea out of hand. She couldn't afford to overlook anything and wouldn't give him *any* opportunity to take her to task. If she didn't manage to make him change his mind about her then it wouldn't be for want of trying!

'What about Leah?' she asked in her most professional tone. 'She will need monitoring throughout the night.'

'She will. However, don't you concern yourself about that. I'll get Kate to sit with her.'

'Fine. I'll say goodnight, then.' Despite her determination, she couldn't keep the hurt from her voice and she saw Jack look at her. She turned away, hating the fact that she was so vulnerable to his comments. She'd never considered herself to be overly sensitive but Jack seemed to have this ability to inflict wounds even though she had no idea why.

'I didn't mean it that way, Meg!' He caught hold of her arm and stopped her when she went to hurry away. His fingers loosely gripped her arm for a moment before he let her go.

'No?' It was impossible to keep the scepticism out of her voice and she heard him sigh.

'No,' he repeated flatly. He ran a hand through his thick black hair then let it fall to his side. 'It would be better if Kate sat with Leah for the rest of the night because you need to get some sleep. These trips are exhausting enough, without you missing out on a full night's sleep into the bargain. Whenever it's necessary we work a shift system as we find it's better to get a couple of hours' sleep rather than none at all.'

'I see. I…I'm sorry if I jumped to conclusions,' she muttered uncomfortably.

'And I'm sorry if I gave you cause to go jumping to them.' Jack's smile was gentle when he looked at her. 'You did a first-rate job tonight, Meg. I appreciate that.'

He turned and walked away, leaving her feeling more confused than ever. If she'd done such a good job, why wouldn't he change his mind about her?

It was impossible to work out the answer because she was too tired to think logically right then. Meg sighed as she followed him back to the huts. Maybe things would be clearer tomorrow after a few hours' sleep, although she doubted it. Where Jack Trent was concerned, feeling confused seemed to be the status quo!

The sun was just rising above the trees when Meg awoke the next morning. She lay quite still for a moment, trying to absorb the thought that she was actually in Africa. It seemed unbelievable that it had happened at last until she remembered the previous night's events.

She scrambled out of bed and pulled on her clothes, grimacing at the feel of the dusty cotton sliding over her skin. She would have dearly loved a fresh change of clothes but, bearing in mind what Jack had said, she hadn't brought all that many with her. It would be better to wait until they reached their destination—where there were bound to be washing facilities—before she got any more dirty.

The village was a hive of activity when she left the hut. Lesley's bed was empty so Meg set about tracking her down to see what she should be doing. She certainly didn't want the rest of the team thinking that she was shirking her share of the work.

'Hi, there! How about a cup of tea?' Lesley smiled when she saw Meg approaching. Picking up a well-worn metal pot from where it was nestling in the fire's embers, she filled a tin cup with dark brown tea and handed it to Meg.

'There's sugar in that tin but make sure you screw the lid back on really tightly or the ants will get in. And there's milk if you fancy it, but it's goat's milk so it is rather an acquired taste, I'm afraid.'

Meg laughed as she crouched down and spooned sugar into the mug. 'You seem to have everything well and truly sorted. I never expected tea in the middle of the bush!'

'Oh, I can do without a lot but not my morning cuppa!' Lesley declared, refilling her own workmanlike mug with the dark brew. She sat on a log, nursing the mug between her hands while she watched Meg cautiously sniff the earthenware jug of milk before adding a little to her tea. 'It isn't that bad once you get used to it.'

Meg took a sip and wrinkled her nose at the unfamiliar taste. 'Hmmm, I'll take your word for that!'

Lesley laughed. 'By the time we leave here you won't even notice the difference! Anyway, what's all this I hear about you and Jack and the exciting night the two of you had?'

'It was rather a baptism of fire,' Meg agreed, taking another swallow of the hot liquid and finding it more palatable this time. 'Still, at least Leah and her baby were both all right in the end. I was so afraid that we wouldn't be able to save them at one point.'

'So Jack told Kate. I believe he said that it was touch and go... Ah, your ears must have been burning—we were just talking about you.' Lesley grinned wickedly as she looked past Meg. 'I bet that's got you worried, hasn't it?'

'It has. I dread to think what you two were saying about me.'

Meg didn't look round even though she knew Jack was standing behind her. She'd heard the mocking note in his voice and wondered if that comment had been aimed at her. Did he think she'd been discussing him with Lesley, asking the other woman why he seemed to have such a downer on her?

The thought that he believed she would be so unprofessional as to do that stung, but she didn't say anything. Disturbing the harmony which so obviously existed within the team was the last thing she wanted to do. However, it hurt to have it brought home to her yet again how Jack viewed her. When he sat beside her, she didn't look round, afraid that he would see from her face that something was wrong. Maybe he'd apologised to her last night *and* told her the truth about why he'd wanted Kate to sit with their patient instead of her, but that didn't mean his attitude towards her had softened in any way!

'Did you sleep OK?'

Meg barely looked up when he addressed her, keeping her eyes firmly fixed on the fire. 'Fine, thank you. How about you?'

'So-so.' He smiled thinly as she shot him a questioning look, unable to resist doing so when she caught the nuance in his voice. 'I was a bit on edge in case I got woken up again. It made me rather…restless.'

Meg buried her nose in her mug, hoping that he wouldn't notice the flush which had turned her cheeks bright red. Jack hadn't been alluding to what had happened when she'd woken him, she assured herself sternly. However, it was far more difficult than it should have been to convince herself.

Unbidden, her mind leapt back to those first few moments after she'd entered his hut the previous night. Suddenly she could recall how warm and smooth his skin had felt beneath her palm, how hard and heavy his body had been when it had pressed hers into the mattress…

She took a hasty swallow of tea then spluttered as it went down the wrong way. Jack took the mug from her hand and thumped her on the back, his grey eyes holding an expression of concern as he watched her struggling for breath.

'Are you all right?' he asked when she finally managed to draw breath.

'I…think…so.' Meg gave one last cough then managed an embarrassed smile, feeling like the world's worst fool. She deserved to choke to death for letting herself start thinking like that!

'I swallowed some tea the wrong way,' she muttered, scrambling to her feet. 'Anyway, I'm fine now so I'll go and see how Leah is. I'm sure Kate could do with a breather.'

She started edging away but Jack stood up as well. 'I'll come with you. There's going to have to be a few changes made to our plans so I may as well get everything sorted out right away.'

He tossed the dregs of his tea into the fire then put the cup on a nearby log. Meg frowned but there was no excuse she could think of to avoid walking with him.

She squared her shoulders, reminding herself how silly it was to start looking for excuses for such an everyday situation as this. She and Jack would be working together over the

coming months so the sooner she got used to the idea the
better it would be. However, that didn't mean she wasn't
deeply aware of him as they crossed the clearing side by side.
It was a relief to enter Leah's hut, and be able to concentrate
on their patient, in fact. Like him or loathe him—and she
wasn't sure yet which it was—it certainly wasn't *easy* to ignore him.

Leah looked tired but radiantly happy when they crouched
down by her bed. She smiled at them, although Meg could tell
that she was in some discomfort. She made a note to ask Jack
if Leah was having any analgesic drugs to minimise the pain
from her operation, although she was sure he would have prescribed some already.

She frowned as she found herself wondering what was going to happen after they left. Leah would need pain relief for
a couple of days at least, not to mention the fact that the
wound would need dressing, and she wasn't sure how they
would deal with that problem.

'You want to see my son?' Leah asked, proudly offering
Jack the baby.

He took the tiny bundle from her and Meg was struck by
how gentle he was as he unwrapped the brightly coloured
shawl in which the infant was swaddled. Jack's hands looked
so large compared to the child's limbs as he carefully examined the little boy, yet there was an innate tenderness about
the way he did it.

It was obvious to Meg that he really cared about this child
and that saving its life had meant an awful lot to him. This
wasn't just a job to Jack—it could never be just that when he
cared so much about the people he treated. The thought simply
increased her admiration for him.

'Well, everything appears to be fine despite the rough ride
this little fellow had, coming into the world!' Jack finished
checking the baby, smiling when he found nothing seriously
wrong with him. Meg knew that difficult births often meant
that an infant could suffer fractures to the clavicle, humerus

or femur, but obviously Jack was confident nothing was amiss. It was a relief to know that.

Once the baby was snugly wrapped in his shawl again, Jack turned his attention to Leah. He quickly examined the incision in her abdomen, frowning when he saw her wince. 'I know it's painful but I'll give you some medicine that will help you.'

He glanced at Meg. 'The wound is my main concern, or at least making sure that it heals well. Infection soon sets in under these conditions and the last thing we want is for that to happen.'

'It will need dressing daily. But it isn't going to be easy to ensure that's done under sterile conditions,' Meg observed worriedly.

'I know. And that's where you come in, Meg.' Jack drew the covers over Leah, before moving away from the bed.

Meg got up and went to join him but her heart was suddenly thumping. She had a horrible feeling that she wasn't going to like what he had to say, although she didn't know why.

Jack glanced towards the bed where a crowd of Leah's relatives was now gathered around her. His face was set when he turned to Meg but that didn't mean she missed the sudden uncertainty in his eyes. Her heart seemed to beat all the harder when she saw it.

'It's obvious that Leah will need careful nursing until we're sure that wound is healing. We simply can't take the risk of it becoming infected by leaving it up to one of her relatives to dress it either.'

He took a deep breath and Meg's hands clenched as she prepared herself for what was to come.

'That's why I've decided that you should stay here with her for the next few days.'

CHAPTER FOUR

'STAY here…?'

Meg's voice tailed off, but Jack must have heard the shock it had held. Taking hold of her arm, he led her outside. He didn't let her go until they were well away from the huts. Did he think she was going to create a scene? Meg wondered giddily. Well, he needn't worry because she was too *stunned* to do that!

'Let's get this straight before we go any further. I didn't make this decision lightly or for any reason other than the fact that I believe it's the best option available in the circumstances.'

Jack's voice grated, although whether from anger because he thought that she was going to disagree with him or what, she had no idea, and didn't waste time trying to work it out. She homed in on what he'd said instead, her head lifting as she stared him straight in the eye.

'In other words, this isn't an attempt to get rid of me—is that what you are trying to say, Jack?' she challenged.

'Yes, that's exactly what I *am* saying!' he bit out before he suddenly sighed. His shoulders rose and fell as he took a deep breath, and this time his tone was far less abrasive.

'I am not trying to get rid of you, Meg. Far from it, in fact. I would have preferred to keep you with us but I really and truly believe that you are by far the best person to take responsibility for Leah's post-operative care. Oh, Lesley and Kate are both excellent nurses but they simply don't have your experience of dealing with post-op patients. That, and that alone, is why I decided that you should be the one to stay on here.'

'I see.'

Funnily enough, she *did* see, and her spirits rose a little. Not that she wasn't still rather stunned by the thought of being left to her own devices in the middle of the bush, of course. However, deep down she knew that she would cope. Jack must have *some* confidence in her if he was prepared to entrust the responsibility for Leah's care to her, and she found herself responding to it.

'So how long do you think I'll need to stay here?' she asked, determined not to give him cause to start having second thoughts. It was a big step for him to have come this far and she certainly didn't want him to start wondering if he'd made the wrong decision.

'Three…maybe four days at the most. As long as there's no sign of infection and you're quite happy with how Leah has responded, the decision will be yours. I've had a word with Moses and he's promised that he'll come back and drive you out to meet us.' Jack suddenly grinned. 'He won't have any problem finding us, of course. It would be impossible to miss a huge steam train so don't worry on that score!'

Meg laughed as well, feeling a little easier now that she was getting used to the idea. 'I won't!' She sobered abruptly. 'But surely this will mean that you'll be under extra pressure by being one member of the team down?'

'It will, but we'll just have to work round it some way or other.' He shrugged. 'One thing you soon discover on these trips is how to adapt as things rarely go as planned.'

'Mmm, I remember you saying something along those lines to Rory last night. I should have taken heed of it!'

She'd meant it as a joke but she saw Jack frown. There was a troubled light in his eyes when he looked at her. 'Look, Meg, if you're at all worried about staying here then say so. It must be quite a daunting prospect when you have absolutely no experience of working in conditions like these so, please, don't think it will go against you.'

'You mean it won't be marked down in the minus column?' she teased, then wondered where she'd found the nerve to ask such a question.

'The minus column?' He looked blank for a second before he grinned. He looked so much younger and so boyishly handsome all of a sudden that her heart gave a small lurch before she brought it sternly under control once more. However, it was hard to control her racing pulse when he treated her to a disturbingly intent look which seemed at odds with the lightness of his tone.

'It's a good idea, actually. I should have thought of it myself. If I made a note of all your good points then a note of any bad ones, it would make it easier, wouldn't it?'

'Easier for what?' she asked, her voice sounding unnaturally husky because it was impossible to remain indifferent when Jack looked at her like that.

'To weigh you up, of course. Work out what makes you tick and decide whether or not you're going to be a useful addition to the team.'

Meg's heart sank as she heard what he said. Maybe he'd tried to pass it off as a joke but it was too close to the truth to pretend he hadn't meant it. She turned away before he saw the hurt which darkened her eyes. So much for thinking that he was starting to see her in a better light!

'I rather think you've already made up your mind about that.'

He caught hold of her arm and stopped her when she went to walk away. 'Look, Meg, I—'

'Hey, Jack, have you got a minute?'

He broke off as Rory called him. Meg saw fleeting indecision cross his face before he let go of her. 'I'd better see what the problem is,' he said shortly. 'I'll check that you have everything you need before we leave.'

'Fine,' Meg said tightly. 'I'd better go and get my bag off the truck, seeing as I'll be staying.'

She headed over to the trucks without a backward glance. Not that she thought Jack would be watching her, of course. He wasn't interested in her except in a purely professional capacity. It wouldn't concern him if she felt hurt or worried or even scared by the thought of staying in the village by herself. So long as he was sure that she would do what was expected of her then that would be enough. Funnily, it didn't seem enough to her. She found herself wishing that Jack would see her not only as a colleague but as a woman. Now, where on earth had that thought sprung from?

'Take care of yourself, kiddo.' Rory gave her a friendly hug. 'If it's any consolation, at least you'll be spared the trauma of having to unpack all the equipment. By the time you arrive everything will be all set up and running perfectly!'

He waggled his bushy eyebrows at her and Meg dutifully laughed. However, she had to admit that now the time had come for the others to depart, she was beginning to feel a little overawed by the prospect of being left on her own.

She forced a smile as Lesley also hugged her warmly. The older woman's face held a trace of concern as she looked at Meg. 'Sure you're OK about this, love? I could have a word with Jack if you're at all worried.'

'No, it's fine. Honestly!' Meg upped her smile a few watts, feigning a nonchalance she wished she felt. 'I'll be perfectly fine here, as you very well know.'

Lesley looked relieved. 'Of course you will. It's just me doing my mother-hen act and clucking over nothing. It drives my kids wild when I fuss over them!' She stepped onto the running-board, ready to haul herself up into the truck. 'See you soon, then!'

With a last wave of her hand, she disappeared inside the cab. Kate waved as well before she climbed up after her. Meg's mouth felt stiff from smiling as she waved them off. Rory must have told the driver to sound his horn because there was the most awful racket before the truck he was in set off as well.

Meg stepped back out of the way as a cloud of dust churned up by the lorries' wheels threatened to engulf her, and gasped when she cannoned into someone standing behind her.

'Sorry…' she began, then found the rest of the apology drying up as she realised it was Jack she'd backed into.

'That's OK.' He treated her to an easy smile before he turned to watch the two trucks disappearing into the trees. 'I just need a couple of minutes to run through everything with you. I've decided to drive myself so I'll soon catch the others up. I thought it would be better in the circumstances if Moses stayed here.'

'I'm sure he won't want to leave Leah at the moment,' she concurred, turning to lead the way back to the village.

'Probably not. However, my main concern was you.' Jack must have seen the start she gave because he smiled. 'I'm not so unfeeling that I don't realise how daunting it must be to stay here on your own, Meg. Apart from Moses and Leah, few of the villagers speak any English.'

He shrugged, looking suddenly *uncomfortable*, if that wasn't too strange a word to use. 'I wanted to be certain that you had someone to turn to if you needed help at any point.'

She was touched by his concern, all the more so because she hadn't expected it. She smiled at him, not trying to disguise the surprise and pleasure she felt. 'Thank you, Jack. I appreciate it.'

He returned her smile, his eyes lingering on the gentle lines of her face as though he couldn't bear to drag them away. Meg felt her pulse leap because there was no doubting the admiration in his eyes. She wasn't vain but she knew that men found her attractive and that many would have called her beautiful. The combination of silky blonde hair, delicate features and a wonderful smile were, to her mind, just a happy combination of genes. Yet suddenly she was glad that Jack found her attractive and it bothered her why it seemed to matter so much.

They were just colleagues…*reluctant* colleagues from Jack's point of view…so why should it matter one way or the other? She had no idea why, she simply knew that it did, and the realisation left her feeling more than a little unsettled. It was a relief when he returned his attention to their patient, quickly and concisely outlining the nursing regime he wanted Meg to follow.

Meg nodded. 'Yes, that's fine. You put Leah on antibiotics immediately as a preventative measure, didn't you?'

'That's right. Obviously, having to operate under non-sterile conditions was a huge risk but there wasn't any choice. I want her kept on the drugs for the next three days at least and then you can review the situation. She'll also need some degree of pain relief as well, so I'll leave you to administer pethidine whenever you feel it necessary. The decision will be yours.'

Meg smiled. 'You were telling the truth when you said that nurses on these trips are nurse *practitioners.*'

'I usually say what I mean, Meg. It saves a lot of trouble at the end of the day, not to mention a great deal of unnecessary confusion.'

Had that been meant as a warning? Was Jack reminding her of all the points he'd made about her lack of suitability for this sort of work? Meg wasn't sure but she took it to heart anyway.

Her shoulders straightened and she looked steadily back at him. 'I'm sure it does. I can't see any point in prevaricating either, although I do believe that often we're forced to re-evaluate a situation because we don't always have all the necessary facts to hand to make a proper assessment in the beginning.'

Jack inclined his head gravely. However, there was a slight curl to his mouth which told her that her words had hit their mark. 'Obviously, we're in agreement, then. So, if you don't have any more questions, I'd better be off. So long as everything is going to plan here, I shall see you in three to four days' time. Someone will come and pick you up.'

He gave her a last brief smile then strode over to the truck and lithely jumped into the cab. Starting the engine with the minimum of fuss, he set off up the track and quickly disappeared into the trees.

Meg's pretty mouth clamped shut with an audible snap. 'Goodbye' would have been nice. 'Take care' even better. And how about a wave? Surely it wouldn't have cost him anything to poke his hand out of the window and wave to her?

She swung round, whipping up her anger at Jack's abrupt departure because she felt so…so *bereft* now that he'd gone! She took a deep breath then, both mentally and physically, squared her shoulders.

To hell with him! She had a job to do and she wasn't going to waste another second *missing* Jack Trent!

'That's great, Leah. It's healing really well.'

Meg smiled as she carefully laid a fresh dressing over the incision in Leah's abdomen. It was the morning of the fourth day of her stay in the village and she was delighted with the progress her patient had made. The wound showed no sign of infection and she'd been able to reduce Leah's pain relief to zero the previous night. It was obvious that everything was going beautifully and she felt a deep sense of personal satisfaction at the thought of a job being well done. It would be something for Jack to put in the plus column…even though it might grieve him to have to do it!

Meg sighed as she picked up a strip of tape to fix the dressing into place, deftly using sterile forceps for the task. Far too often thoughts of Jack had intruded during the past few days. He seemed to have got well and truly under her skin so that the last thing she saw each night before she went to sleep was an image of his face.

That was bad enough, but he also kept cropping up at the most inopportune moments throughout the day, like now, for instance, when she simply wanted to get on with her job. What on earth was wrong with her?

There was no answer to that question so Meg put it out of her mind as she picked up a second strip of tape. She had instigated the most rigorously sterile routine she could think of to dress Leah's wound, and it had paid off, although she knew that the villagers thought she was mad!

All the washing and scrubbing, the boiling and gloving-up was a daily ritual which now attracted a large audience. Meg was aware that it had fast become the highlight of everyone's day but she didn't mind because it had helped enormously to break the ice.

In the past few days she'd treated three children with cuts to their arms or feet and an old woman with a weeping ulcer on her leg. Give her a bit longer and she could set up her own general practice! she thought ruefully, peeling off her gloves and depositing them in the waste container. However, if nothing else, it had boosted her confidence. Despite what Jack thought, she could handle this type of work.

She groaned under her breath when she realised that she'd arrived back where she'd started and was thinking about Jack once more. If only she could press a button and delete all thoughts of him, life would be so much easier! she decided as she picked up Leah's son for their daily cuddle. He stared at her unblinkingly, his dark eyes as big as saucers as he tried to focus on her face.

'You're a real little sweetheart, aren't you?' Meg crooned, buzzing his fuzz of black hair with a kiss as she snuggled him close to her breast. His mouth opened and he immediately started searching for a nipple to latch onto as she laughed.

'No joy there, I'm afraid, young man! You need your mum for that.'

She looked up with the smile still lingering on her lips as someone came into the hut, and felt her heart come to an abrupt halt when she saw Jack. His unexpected arrival stole her ability to speak so that she could only stand and stare at him until the baby began to grizzle when he realised that the promised meal hadn't materialised.

Meg passed him back to Leah, using the few seconds it took to try and get herself in hand. What a waste of time that was! Her heart was thumping, her pulse playing tick with itself, her whole body a shivery mass of nerves. Damn the wretched man for making her act like a mindless moron and thereby reinforcing everything he thought about her!

The thought was just enough to unlock her voice, and she rounded on him, unaware that annoyance had added an extra sparkle to her bright blue eyes. 'What are you doing here? Dic you decide to check up on me and make sure I wasn't making a hash of things?'

Colour swept up his face, yet Meg could tell in an instant that it wasn't anger that had caused it. Her mouth dropped open as she realised that there was *embarrassment* written all over his handsome face. Why? Because she'd sussed him out? Or…or for some other reason? It was that last itsy-bitsy thought that made her heart surge back to life.

'I…er…ahem!' He coughed, trying to pretend that it was dust in his throat which had made him stop. However, Meg— with a new-found insight she couldn't have explained even if she'd written a whole *thesis* on it—knew it was a ruse. Jack didn't know what to say and the thought of this superbly confident man being at a loss for words struck her dumb as well so that they both stood and stared at each other.

Jack recovered first, although not before he'd cleared his throat a second time. 'Ahem…I haven't come to check up on you,' he bit out.

Meg's eyebrows seemed to be the only bit of her willing to work at that moment so she used them to full effect. They swooped upwards in silent, sceptical query, saying more clearly than she could ever have done how she felt about that statement.

If anything, Jack's colour deepened, a dark flush now staining both his face and neck. He uttered what might—or might not—have been an oath and swung round, striding out of the hut without a backward glance.

Meg stared at the empty doorway then blinked a few times, wondering if her poor addled wits had finally thrown in the towel. Had she imagined that he'd been here? Had she conjured up not only his face but his body and his voice this time?

Leah, lying in the bed, giggled. Meg looked at her blankly, seeing the amusement that touched the other woman's face as Leah gave her a shy smile. 'Your man was pleased to see you but did not want to show it, I think.'

She sighed as she nestled the hungry baby to her breast.

'Dr Jack is like Moses. He does not want you to think he is weak by showing how much he has missed you.'

'Missed me?' Meg echoed, then shook her head. 'Oh, no, I don't think…'

She swallowed hard as the possibility hit her. Jack had missed her? Could it be true? Was that why he'd acted so strangely and been so…so *embarrassed*?

She wasn't even aware that she was moving until she found herself outside the hut. It was still early morning but the heat was already intense, the sun a glowing yellow ball beating down on her. Shading her eyes, she looked around but there was no sign of Jack. Surely he hadn't left?

She hurried across the clearing, uncaring of the curious looks she attracted. There were few places to hide and she knew all of them by now. There was the stream the women used to wash their clothes in and the pool they used to bathe in and that was it. It was a toss-up which to choose but in the end she opted for the latter and hurried along the path that led to it.

She was out of breath by the time the pool came in sight and more than willing to stop even before she saw Jack sitting hunched up on a rock near to where the water gushed from a fissure in the side of the cliff. Her heart started fluttering inside her ribs like a caged bird as she studied him. He looked…well, lost, if that was the right word, and she wasn't sure that it was. For a moment she wondered if she'd been mad to follow him but the thought of leaving him to sit there on his own was more than she could bear.

'Mind if I sit down?'

'Be my guest.'

His voice was level to a fault, the look he gave her equally bland, and her heart sank. This was *Dr* Jack Trent before her now, not the man who'd stalked out of that hut a few minutes earlier, a man who'd looked as though he might just have a few human emotions left inside him! Missed her? Huh!

She plucked disconsolately at a blade of grass, wishing she could think of an opening, but her mind was blank. It was left to Jack to open the conversation, which he did in his most irritating tone.

'Before we go any further, I want to make it clear that I didn't come back to check up on you.' His face was as animated as a lump of granite as he looked coldly at her. 'If I hadn't thought you were up to the job then I wouldn't have asked you to stay here.'

'Shall I take that as a compliment?' Where had that smart-aleck question sprung from? Meg wondered sickly, watching his mouth curl disdainfully.

'That's up to you, I imagine,' he shot back.

'Thank you.' Her tongue seemed to be running away with her, out of her control and off on a mission of its own. Meg tried clamping her lips together but there was no stopping it. 'It's always nice to be appreciated. It makes one feel valued, doesn't it?'

'Meaning what?' he demanded icily.

'Meaning anything you want it to mean, of course.' She just managed to stop herself from actually adding *Touché* but she knew he'd mentally filled it in anyway. Her toes curled with mortification as she realised how childish it was to sit there, bickering like that. But he'd started it!

Jack suddenly laughed and Meg's eyes flew to his face, widening in shock when she saw the amusement that was etched into every craggy line. 'You have an answer for everything, don't you, Meg Andrews? I don't recall *that* fact being on your CV!'

'Maybe you didn't check it over clearly enough?' she suggested, smiling back at him because it was impossible to remain aloof. Did he have any idea how handsome and desirable he looked when he laughed? she wondered, rapidly taking note of those salient points herself. She doubted it, otherwise he would have laughed more often and been snapped up by some discerning woman years ago! Still, that woman's loss was *her* gain...

It was definitely time to call a halt to that thought. She frowned when Jack shook his head bemusedly. 'What?'

'Nothing. Everything. I don't know what to say. I can't recall ever having this trouble with anyone before. How do you manage to make things so bloody complicated, Meg?'

Now there was a question, one she wouldn't touch with the proverbial bargepole! Did he really think she would be fool enough to hand him ammunition like that?

She smiled sweetly and heard him sigh. 'Daft question. Forget it. Anyway, to get back to why I'm here—the answer's simple. I decided that it would be better if I came for you in something more comfortable than that old bone-shaker of a truck.'

He rose to his feet, offering her his hand as he grinned down at her. 'I thought you deserved better than that after being left here all on your own, so I managed to borrow something a bit more luxurious. Come and see.'

Meg placed her hand in his and let him haul her to her feet, laughing to cover how touched she felt that he should have gone to any trouble on her behalf. 'The mind boggles at the thought of what you could have found in the middle of the bush! What is it?'

'You'll see. Come on.'

Jack led her back to the village, skirting the perimeter as he headed for a thin stand of trees. Meg gasped when she saw a dark green Land Rover parked beneath them.

'Where on earth did you get it?' she demanded, turning to him in astonishment.

'It wasn't easy. It took a lot of careful negotiating.' His eyes danced as he watched her run an incredulous hand over the vehicle's dusty paintwork. It was several years old but in immaculate condition for all that, and she couldn't for the life of her work out how he'd come by it.

'Come on, Jack, tell me where you got it,' she wheedled, and heard him laugh softly. It was odd the kind of effect a laugh could have, she found herself thinking as a frisson flashed down her spine. But that depended on who had actually done the laughing, of course…

'So Richard immediately offered to let me use it to fetch

you. He said it was the least he could do after all we're doing for him.'

'Richard?' she queried huskily, then gave herself a mental shake. Snap out of it, Andrews! Get a grip before he starts thinking you're a half-wit!

'The ruler of Oncamba. Oh, his tribal name is something I can't pronounce, but as he's happy for us to call him by the name he's used for the last twenty years, that isn't a problem.'

Jack's mouth pursed as he stared reflectively at the dusty vehicle. 'It must have been a huge adjustment for Richard, coming back to Oncamba to live when he'd left the country as a child. I really admire the way he's put his heart and soul into improving the quality of life here for the people. He's a great guy and I'm sure you'll like him, Meg.'

'I'm sure I shall. I like him already, in fact. The thought of not having to bounce around in that rust-bucket of a truck is like winning the lottery!'

She grinned, wanting to lighten the mood because she wasn't ready to handle this situation which seemed to be developing all of a sudden. Was she attracted to Jack? Yes. Physically or mentally? Both. So how was she going to deal with it? She had no idea.

She rushed on before her mind could toss up any more disturbing questions. 'So, do I take it that we're leaving this morning?'

'If you're quite happy with Leah's progress, then yes. It'll take a few hours before we catch up with the others. We've already made two stops and I'll bring you up to date on what's happened as we drive. However, the sooner we leave the sooner we'll get things back on track again…if you'll excuse the pun!'

Meg rolled her eyes. 'That was terrible! Still, I'll let you off, seeing as you've gone to all this trouble on my behalf. I'll just need to sort out my things… Oh, seeing as you're here, would you take a look at a couple of patients I've been treating?'

'Patients?' Jack's brows rose and for a moment she wondered if maybe she'd overstepped her authority. But there was no way that she could have refused to help the villagers—her conscience wouldn't have let her do that even if Jack wasn't pleased about it. She had a duty to care for the sick, and nobody—not even Jack Trent—was going to stop her doing that!

'Yes,' Meg said firmly. 'There were people who needed medical attention in the village so I treated them.'

'Fine. I'll be happy to give a second opinion, Meg.' He glanced at his watch. 'We'll aim to leave here by eleven, then, if you think that will give us enough time.'

He was actually deferring to her? Meg's heart swelled as she realised it. It was hard to contain her happiness as she led the way back to the village and asked Moses to round up her 'patients'. Maybe it was only a small step but added to all the others Jack seemed to have taken already that day it seemed that she was making tremendous progress. When Jack agreed with everything she'd done to treat the various injuries, she felt as though she were floating on air.

It was in that happy frame of mind that she packed up her belongings and said goodbye, although there was a lump in her throat when it came to taking her leave of Leah and her baby son. Meg knew that she would never forget them and hoped that one day she would be able to go back and visit them, a wish reiterated by Moses when he shook her hand.

'Thank you, Dr Meg. Thank you for everything you have done.'

'You're very welcome. Just mind that you take good care of Leah and that beautiful little boy of yours,' she replied huskily.

All the villagers came out to wave them off. Meg waved until her arm ached before she sank back in her seat as they rounded a bend and the village disappeared from sight. 'I'll miss them. Even though we couldn't really speak to each other, I still feel that we got on well together.'

'That's because you have a natural empathy with people.' Jack shrugged as he set the vehicle into four-wheel-drive while they traversed a partially dried-up river bed. 'You don't need a common language to show people that you care about them.'

It seemed that the compliments were coming thick and fast now, and Meg basked in them. Jack seemed to have changed his mind about her and it felt as though a load had been lifted off her shoulders. He kept up an easy conversation as they drove, bringing her up to date with what had happened, treating her as he would have treated any colleague, in fact—as someone he valued for the contribution she was going to make. It all added to the feel-good factor so that by the time they reached the end of their journey several hours later, Meg was barely aware of feeling tired.

Jack drew the Land Rover to a halt on a small rise above the railway track and stopped the engine. There was a note of pride in his deep voice as he pointed to the valley below.

'Well, there it is. The *Oncamba Angel*. What do you think?'

'It's fantastic!' Meg couldn't think of a more suitable word than that. To see the train sitting there in the hot afternoon sun, its deep red paintwork shining, its brass gleaming, *was* pure fantasy!

Beyond the railway track the land lay in shades of umber and green, offset by the purplish haze of mountains in the distance. The last time she'd seen a train like the *Oncamba Angel* had been on a television screen when she'd watched a repeat of the film *The Railway Children*, a childhood favourite of hers. Now she had to pinch herself to prove that she wasn't dreaming.

She didn't say anything as Jack started the vehicle again and drove them down the steep incline. Meg climbed out as soon as they'd stopped and headed straight for the train, eager to see inside it. There was a queue of people near one of the doors, patiently waiting to be seen, and she smiled when they moved aside so that she could board the train. It was obvious that surgeries were under way and she paused to get her bearings, not wanting to go barging in and disturbing anyone. Jack had stopped to speak to someone so she decided it would be better to wait for him before she went exploring.

'Oh, hi! You must be Meg. I'm Alison Graham, the radi-ologist-cum-lab technician-cum-general dogsbody. Welcome on board!'

Meg swung round at the sound of the cheery greeting and smiled at the plump, little dark-haired woman who had come out of one of the rooms. She opened her mouth to reply when it suddenly hit her that Alison was staring at her as though she'd seen a ghost.

'Is something wrong?' Meg asked instead, frowning as she took stock of the other woman's startled expression.

'I…um. Sorry. You just reminded me of someone else, that's all.' Alison looked embarrassed as she offered Meg her hand.

Meg shook it but she was curious to know what could have prompted such a reaction. 'Really? Who?'

Alison laughed shortly. 'Oh, it's ridiculous, really! I mean she would *never* have been seen dead in a place like this so I can't imagine why I thought you were Briony! Must need my eyes checked!'

Meg laughed dutifully but her curiosity was still aroused. 'Briony? Is she a friend of yours, then?'

'Well, no, not really. I mean, I'm sure she was very nice but I didn't really know her all that well…'

She tailed off uncomfortably then took a deep breath and hurried on, 'Briony was Jack's wife, you see. You must have heard of her—Briony James, the model? They got divorced a couple of years ago and, to be honest, I think it hit him hard because he was crazy about her, even though she was an ab-solute bitch to him. Still, that's the way of the world, isn't it? It's no wonder that it's put him off women, especially beau-tiful ones… Oh, no offence intended, of course. I'm sure Jack doesn't let his personal feelings influence him in a work sit-uation.'

Alison looked as though she were choking on hot chestnut as she tried to undo any damage she might have caused. Meg fixed the smile to her mouth which was in danger of becoming a permanent affliction. It wasn't poor Alison's fault if she had, unwittingly, touched on the truth!

'I'm sure he doesn't,' she agreed levelly, while her mind said something entirely different. Did Jack see her in the same light as his ex-wife? Was that the real explanation behind his animosity? She had a horrible feeling that Alison might have got to the crux of the problem.

'Right. I'll show you where everything is then you can get settled in.'

Jack came on board and Alison muttered a hasty greeting then hurried away after sending a beseeching look in Meg's direction. Obviously, the subject of Briony James was a no-go area but Alison needn't have worried that she would mention it. She wasn't that silly! However, Meg knew that what she'd learned was going to haunt her. Making Jack change his mind about her was going to be harder than ever if he was set on comparing her to his ex-wife!

CHAPTER FIVE

'IF YOU would wait in here…thank you.'

Meg ushered the young woman into the coach which had been fitted out as a waiting room. There were already a dozen people in there, waiting to be seen. It had been non-stop since they'd set up shop at a little after seven that morning and, from the look of the queue outside, it was going to be another busy day.

It was a week since she'd boarded the train and each day had been hectic. The sheer number of people who had turned up had amazed Meg at first but she'd soon adapted to the situation. However, it did mean that there wasn't a minute to spare each day, no bad thing to her mind as it meant she was too busy to start worrying over what she'd learned about Jack's broken marriage. Work was all she had time for and that was the way she liked it.

'Give her a number and put her down for a general check-up as well as a cervical examination,' she instructed the young woman clerk who'd been sent along to help them on this leg of their journey. Her name was Lavinia and she'd proved herself invaluable by acting as interpreter as well as maintaining their records. Now she gave Meg her usual calm smile.

'Of course, Dr Meg. Is Dr Jack ready for his next patient yet?'

Meg glanced over her shoulder and shook her head when she saw that the consulting-room door was still closed. She'd been surprised when Jack had told her that she would be working with him, because she'd expected him to choose either Lesley or Kate. The cynical thought that maybe he wanted to keep an eye on her had been firmly squashed because she'd known how unproductive it would be to think along those lines. She couldn't work properly, believing that someone was looking over her shoulder and always checking up on her.

In the event, she'd discovered that she'd been right to dismiss it because there had been no hint that Jack lacked confidence in her. Quite the opposite, in fact, because it had soon become apparent that they worked well together. However, Meg was aware that things could change very quickly and took care always to be on her toes around him. There was no room for complacency where Jack Trent was concerned!

Now she quietly went back to the consulting room, pausing for a moment while her eyes adjusted to the dim lighting. Jack had seen a number of patients with serious eye problems since they'd arrived at this location, and the man who'd turned up that morning was yet another one.

Meg made her way quietly to the examination couch, watching intently as Jack tilted the patient's head to the side and shone a small light into his left eye. She heard him sigh softly and knew that once again he'd found something seriously wrong.

'Lights, please, Meg,' he said levelly, snapping off his torch as she turned the lights up to their full setting. The train had its own generator and water filtration system, making it virtually self-contained. Although conditions were a bit cramped, they were far better than Meg had expected. The two small operating theatres were state of the art, most of the equipment having been donated by an American company that fitted out hospitals throughout the world.

Drugs and other medical supplies had been donated by a number of high-profile companies throughout Europe, while a small British firm had sent out a team of highly skilled workmen to fit and refurbish the train. Two of the men were qualified engineers and they'd got the engine up and running. They'd stayed on and were acting as their driver and mechanic for the journey. They were also training four Oncamban men to take over their jobs when they returned to Britain.

Meg was impressed by the generosity of all those people who'd helped get the operation under way but she knew that none of it would have happened if it hadn't been for Jack's determination. He had been the driving force behind it all and her admiration for him knew no bounds because of that.

Now she moved away from the couch when he murmured that he would like a word with her. She waited until they were out of earshot of the patient. 'I take it there's a problem?'

'Yes, unfortunately. Another case of severe trachoma,' he said tersely. 'Damn! It's worse than I thought.'

She knew that he wasn't referring solely to the case he'd just seen. The number of cases of the severe eye infection they'd seen in the past few days had startled her because she'd had no idea it was such a huge problem. The infection was spread either by flies or through direct contact with another sufferer, and began with conjunctivitis which grew worse through not being treated.

The sufferer's eyes then became very inflamed and the conjunctiva, the transparent membrane which covers the white of the eye and lines the inside of the eyelids, would thicken and roughen with scar tissue. Damage to the mucus-secreting cells and tear ducts meant that the eye became very dry, exacerbating the problem. Often the patients upper eyelid would become so scarred that it rolled inwards, causing the eyelashes to rub against the cornea. The constant irritation led to secondary infection and ulceration and the end result was loss of vision.

'Isn't there anything you can do to help him?' Meg asked sadly, glancing over her shoulder at their patient.

Jack shook his head and his voice was laced with frustration. 'No. The cornea in the right eye is too badly damaged It would need a corneal graft to restore his sight. I might be able to do something about the left one if I operate to correct the lid deformities.'

He sighed as he ran a weary hand round the back of his neck. 'It might be too late even now, but I'll give it a shot It's his only hope if he isn't going to lose his sight completely.'

Meg nodded. 'I'll add him to the list and get Lavinia to explain everything to him. The usual antibiotics?'

Jack smiled. 'Yep, why not? They might help, although I doubt it. Still, it makes me feel that at least I'm doing *something*!'

'You're doing everything you can, Jack,' she said sternly, hating to hear him sounding so downhearted. 'You're a doctor, not a miracle worker!'

'Yes, ma'am!' His smile took any sting out of the words, and Meg laughed.

'That's better! It's about time you realised what a great job you're doing here,' she declared.

'If I am then it's because I've got such a good team with me,' he replied in a tone which made her inwardly melt. There was a new spring to her step as she escorted the patient out and explained to Lavinia what was happening so she could relay it to him.

Did Jack now believe that she was a useful addition to his team? she wondered as she went to collect their next patient, a young mother with a six-year-old girl in tow who was obviously suffering from an eye infection.

She ushered the pair into the consulting room and got the child settled on the couch while Jack washed his hands. Maybe he did. The thought naturally pleased her. However, as she stepped aside so that he could examine his small patient, she knew deep down that it hadn't had quite the impact it might have had in the beginning.

So what did she want from Jack? she wondered, handing him a fresh pair of latex gloves from the box. She wasn't sure but it was unsettling to realise that she still wanted more than she already had.

The soft sounds of the night were soothing after the noise and bustle of the day. Meg stood on the platform at the rear of the train and let her eyes adjust to the darkness. Behind her, the carriage they used through the day as a waiting room and as a communal lounge at night was softly lit by lamps. She heard a burst of laughter as Rory came to the end of one of his impossibly complicated jokes and smiled, although she had no desire to go back inside and join in the fun. It had been a busy day and she felt like a few minutes on her own to draw breath.

'Oops, sorry!' Alison stopped dead as she and her husband, Guy, the other surgeon on board, came out of the carriage and spotted Meg. 'We didn't mean to disturb you.'

'Don't be silly,' Meg said at once, smiling at the young couple. She liked them both and admired the fact that they'd put their lives on hold while they came on this trip. They both worked at a hospital in Leeds and this was their third overseas aid mission to date. Alison's bubbly, slightly scatty manner was in direct contrast to Guy's more sober approach to life, but it was obvious they were crazy about one another. Meg suddenly found herself envying them.

She'd had plenty of boyfriends but there had never been anyone really *special*, the Mr Right who would make her life complete. Would she ever meet the man who was capable of doing that? she wondered, then found her mind turning to thoughts of Jack before she could stop it.

A wash of colour ran up her face and she quickly turned to look out across the darkened countryside, although there was little danger that Alison and Guy would notice it, let alone correctly interpret its cause. Thoughts like that were ridiculous, yet she couldn't seem to rid herself of it no matter how hard she tried. It was as though all the questions she hadn't asked when Alison had first told her about Jack's wife were suddenly demanding answers. Foolish or not, suddenly she knew that she had to know more!

'It's beautiful here at night, isn't it?' she said casually, inwardly cringing at her own guile. Where had she learned how to be so…so underhand? Heaven knew, but, then, thoughts of heaven weren't uppermost in her mind!

'I bet you two enjoy being together on these trips, don't you?'

'Oh, yes, it's great, isn't it, Guy?' Alison put an affectionate arm through her husband's in an unselfconscious show of affection. 'I'd hate it if Guy went away by himself, which is why I volunteered to work for the agency.'

'Mmm, I can imagine how much you would miss one another,' Meg said with an understanding smile. 'It must put a lot of strain on a marriage when one partner goes off overseas for a long time. Is that why Jack and his wife split up, by any chance?'

Alison took the bait. 'Oh, I don't think so, not really. Of course, I could be speaking out of turn, but I think there were *other* problems.'

'I don't think we should start speculating, Ali,' Guy said quickly, obviously uncomfortable. 'After all, it was only hearsay…'

'Hearsay, my foot! That woman had more men than I've had hot dinners! What Jack saw in her I'll never know.' Alison was really getting into her stride now. Her voice rose in direct proportion to her indignation.

'Oh, she was beautiful—still is, in fact—but beauty is as beauty does, as my gran used to say. From what I heard, Briony had one affair after the other until Jack simply got tired of being made a fool of. Whether he instigated the split I'm not sure, because he never talks about it, but we were all glad he was rid of her. Briony James was trouble with a capital T! It's just such a damned shame that he's taken it so—'

Alison broke off, a look of horror crossing her pretty face as she stared at a spot directly behind Meg. Meg felt a frisson run down her spine and stiffened. She didn't need to look round to know that Jack was standing behind her. She could *feel* him there, feel his eyes boring holes in her back, feel his anger…

'Am I allowed to add my ten pence worth? Or would you prefer to discuss my private life amongst yourselves?'

His voice grated with anger and some other emotion that made Meg wince. The pain she could hear in it made her want to put her arms around him and hug him, only she knew what a mistake that would be! It took her all her strength to look at him as he stepped between them, staring from Alison to

Guy before finally letting his gaze settle on her. His cold grey eyes meshed with hers in a look that tore her composure to shreds before he turned away as though he couldn't bear the sight of her.

'Obviously, you're all extremely interested in what went on so I may as well tell you the full story.'

He smiled but there wasn't a trace of amusement in the taut curling of his lips and Meg felt even worse. He was angry and upset, as he had a right to be, but he was also hurt, and that fact alone caused her such pain that it was hard to remain standing there and witness it. Obviously, he still loved his ex-wife deeply and the realisation was the worst punishment he could have inflicted on her, although she wasn't sure why.

'Briony did, indeed, have several affairs during the two years we were married, although I doubt there were as many as my *friends* believe.'

Guy flinched at that. 'Look, Jack, I don't—'

Jack didn't appear to have heard him because he didn't pause. Guy fell silent in embarrassment.

'At first I tried to pretend nothing was wrong but that wasn't what Briony wanted. She has a great love of drama, you see, and positively thrives on confrontational situations—the arguments, the recriminations, the tears and then making up afterwards. You must know what I mean even if you haven't experienced it yourselves.'

Jack looked round expectantly but nobody said anything so he shrugged and carried on. 'However, it got to the point where I don't think either of us could be bothered playing the same old scene time after time so we decided to call it a day. I suppose I could try to analyse why it didn't work out for us. Was it my fault for being so tied up in my work that I couldn't give her the attention she yearned? That sort of thing. But I don't want to bore you. Just believe me when I say that I've learned a lot from the experience and let's leave it at that, eh?'

He smiled around at them, even responded pleasantly when Alison muttered something unintelligible before she scurried back inside, dragging an abject-looking Guy after her. Meg took a deep breath but there didn't seem to be any way to erase the shame she felt. It had been unforgivable to go delving into Jack's personal life like that, even worse to have involved poor Alison the way she had. If nothing else, she had to explain to Jack that the other woman wasn't to blame, even though she quailed at the thought.

'Please, don't blame Alison for what happened,' she said, her voice trembling because it was so hard to admit that she was responsible for such a blatant invasion of his privacy. 'I...I asked her about your marriage.'

'I'm flattered. I didn't realise that you were so interested in my failed love life, Meg. I do hope I managed to answer all your questions. I mean, if there's anything else you'd like to know then don't be shy—ask away.'

Her cheeks flamed with mortification as she felt the lash of his tongue. She deserved to feel like that, though, and wouldn't flinch from admitting she was at fault, even though she knew he would use it against her.

'I was wrong to go delving into things that don't concern me, Jack. I apologise.'

He gave a soft little laugh yet she heard the dangerous edge it held. 'And you think that makes everything right again, do you?'

She shrugged, striving for a modicum of composure. The rest of the party were only a few feet away inside the carriage so there was nothing to be scared of. Yet the way Jack was looking at her didn't exactly settle her mind. 'I'm sure it doesn't. But I really and truly am sorry, Jack. I don't know what else I can say.'

She looked round as a noise alerted her to the fact that the others were heading off to their compartments for the night. The lights went out inside the carriage, plunging it into darkness. There was just the dim overhead light above the platform left on now to see by, and she felt her nerves tighten as Jack took a slow step towards her.

His face looked as though it had been carved from stone as he stared down at her, his eyes as though they'd been leached

of all warmth. 'Neither do I, Meg. But there must be a better
way that a beautiful woman like you can atone for her mistakes. Briony was full of good ideas, believe me.'

'I'm not Briony!' She heard the plea in her voice but she
wasn't sure that Jack either heard or took heed of it. Her heart
was thumping like mad as he took another slow step towards
her. He looked neither angry nor sad, she realised sickly. In
fact, he looked completely devoid of emotion as he slid his
hand behind her neck and pulled her towards him, and it was
that discovery which stopped her pulling away. To see Jack
looking so…so *empty* was more than she could bear!

His lips were cool and hard and totally lacking in feeling
when they settled on hers. They did all the right things but for
all the wrong reasons, and Meg felt tears spill from her eyes.
It was the most emotionless kiss she'd ever experienced and
it hurt her unbearably to know that anyone was capable of
feeling like that. She would far rather that Jack had kissed her
in anger, in disgust, in loathing, in…in *any* other way than
that! Maybe that was what made her do what she did next.

He'd started to draw back when Meg reached up and twined
her arms around his neck, abruptly stopping him from moving
away from her. She felt him stiffen, heard the soft indrawn
breath he took and felt a fierce elation rocket through her that
at last he'd shown some sign of emotion. She had to stand on
tiptoe to reach his mouth but as soon as her lips touched his
she knew it had been worth the effort. There was a fire beneath
the chill now, a pliancy which hadn't been there seconds before. Maybe he wasn't a completely lost cause after all.

She pressed her mouth to his and kissed him with every
scrap of emotion she could summon up, not caring what it was
because anything was better than nothing. If he had no feelings
left then she would give him some of hers, warm him, comfort
him, anger or please him by simple osmosis!

'Meg!' Her name was muffled by her own mouth as he tried
to speak. She wouldn't let him. Her hands were urgent now
as they clung to his neck, feeling the silky hair at his nape
tickling her palms. It was a strain standing on her toes so she

was forced to steady herself by leaning against him, and she felt the very instant his body surged to life. It shocked her as much as it obviously shocked him.

He thrust her away from him with a muttered oath. In the dim light his face was all hard angles, his grey eyes blazing as he glared at her. 'What the hell do you think you're doing?'

He sounded like an offended virgin and the comparison was so ridiculous that she almost laughed out loud, although it really wasn't anything to laugh about. Deep down she knew that come the morning she was going to regret what she'd done tonight, but the morning seemed an awful long way off right then.

'Trying to see if you're human, that's all.' She tilted her head and looked at him steadily, watching the tide of colour that swept up his face.

'I think you just got your answer, then, don't you?' he shot back. He gave a throaty laugh and his eyes mocked her. 'So what happens next? I might not be up for a long-term relationship but I'm open to offers, Meg, if that's what this is all about.'

It was her turn to flush then, as he called her bluff. It was an effort not to squirm when he continued to look at her expectantly. 'It's not!' she declared hotly.

'Then I suggest you think first before you go throwing yourself at a man again. He might not be the gentleman that I am.' He calmly opened the carriage door, but if he thought he was getting away with that after she'd been trying to help him he could think again!

'I might not want *him* to be a gentleman, though!'

Jack hesitated, only for a second admittedly, but it was enough to tell her the jibe had hit its mark. Meg counted to ten then added another ten for good measure before she followed him inside. How did she know that she was going to pay for that last remark and pay dearly?

She crept into her compartment and climbed into her bunk. Drawing the sheet up to her chin, she lay in the darkness and tried to work out how she felt about that idea. A little bit worried. A little unnerved. But basically quite happy.

She rolled onto her side and closed her eyes with a sigh of contentment. All right, so maybe she *was* mad but she'd achieved something. Even knowing that Jack was annoyed enough to give her hell, that was better than knowing he couldn't have cared less!

On that oddly comforting thought she slept.

Hell wasn't the word for it, Meg thought sourly the next morning. Jack hadn't given her a moment's peace since they'd started work, picking fault with everything she did. If World War Three had suddenly broken out in sub-Saharan Africa no doubt he'd blame her for it. Flood, fire, famine, plague, not to mention swarms of locusts, she was single-handedly responsible for all the ills which had ever beset mankind!

'For heaven's sake, how long does it take to pass that damned scalpel, woman?'

'Sir!' Meg snapped it into his hand, her eyes flashing dangerously above her mask.

'Are you trying to be funny, Staff Nurse Andrews?' he demanded, making an infinitely delicate incision in the patient's upper eyelid.

'Of course not, sir.' She caught Rory's eyes and drew her finger across her throat in comic mime. It was just unfortunate that Jack happened to glance up at that moment.

'This is an operating theatre, Staff, not kindergarten. I suggest you try remembering that.' He turned cold eyes on Rory. 'That goes for you too, Dr O'Donnell.'

'Sir!'

They both snapped out the word in unison and Meg saw Jack stiffen before he made an obvious effort to focus on what he was doing. However, that didn't mean she believed he was going to overlook her lapses, either those of the previous night or those of that day. She had committed the ultimate sin by making Jack admit that he'd wanted her, and she would pay for it, one way...or another!

A frisson ran down her spine and she bit her lip, glad that the concealing mask hid her expression. At some point during her sleep she'd found herself dreaming about him and the memory was infinitely disturbing as it came sharply back to her. It was an effort to keep her mind on what they were doing rather than let it go spinning off again along that erotic path. However, she was too much of a professional to put a patient at risk by not giving one hundred per cent concentration to her work. Maybe Jack should put that in his plus column?

The operation went well and, at the end of it Meg knew that Jack was as pleased as he could be with what he'd achieved. He'd been operating on the man they'd seen the previous day, Benjamin Asadu, and although it hadn't been possible to restore the sight in his right eye at least he would retain the sight in his left.

Jack put the last delicate stitch into the patient's eyelid then stepped away from the operating table. 'That's it, then. Not too bad a job, all things considered.'

Meg carefully covered the man's eye with sterile gauze and gently bandaged it in place, her movements deft and precise as she worked. Rory was busily reversing the anaesthetic, constantly monitoring the readings from the bank of equipment beside him.

He unhooked the patient from the monitors at last then wheeled the trolley Benjamin was lying on to the door. Kate would be ready to receive him as she was acting as post-op nurse that day, caring for the patients Jack and Guy sent to the recovery bay. Most would be free to go home after a few hours, although some, like Benjamin, would be given repeat appointments and be seen on their return journey through the area in a few weeks' time.

Meg knew that it would have been better if they could have kept closer tabs on each patient they operated on, but it was impossible to do that in the circumstances. There were teams of volunteers from various aid agencies working throughout Oncamba and Jack had arranged for some of them to supervise their patients' care.

It was far from ideal but the best they could do, and it seemed to be working well enough from the reports they'd had back. Where work was concerned, Jack had everything sewn up. It was only his personal life that seemed to have great big holes in it…

'Drat!' Meg swore softly as she dropped the kidney dish containing the instruments that needed sterilising. She cursed the fact that she hadn't been concentrating properly as she bent to pick them up. She knew that Jack was watching her but she ignored him. However, it was hard to disregard the biting note in his voice as he berated her for her clumsiness.

'You seem to be having trouble focusing on work today, Staff. Either get yourself together or ask Lesley to swop with you.'

He elbowed the swing door to the scrub room open, pausing to add a rider to the less-than-friendly piece of advice. 'There's no room on this trip for those who aren't totally committed to the job.'

The doors snapped shut and Meg straightened at a rush. She had the kidney dish in her hand and for one second actually considered hurling it after him. Her fingers tightened around the metal container as she took a steadying breath.

It would be an unforgivable breech of protocol to do that. Jack would be quite within his rights to send her back to England. Was that what he was hoping for, by any chance? That he could rid himself of her annoying presence and still come up smelling of roses? No way!

Meg took the instruments to the autoclave to be sterilised then set about cleaning up the operating theatre. It had been decided that they would do the cleaning in the theatres themselves to be absolutely certain that sterile conditions were adhered to. She worked quickly but carefully, making sure that everything was ready for their next patient, although, as far as she knew, Jack didn't have another operation scheduled that day.

She frowned as she left the theatre, wondering what his plans were and if he intended to see more patients that afternoon. He hadn't mentioned anything about their schedule for that day but, then, he'd been too busy taking pot-shots at her all morning to hold a civilised conversation!

Meg sighed as she stripped off her gown and dumped it in the basket. Would Jack ever forgive her for what she'd done the night before? Maybe he could have overlooked her nosiness in digging into his private life but what about the way she'd acted afterwards by kissing him like that?

Her heart performed a couple of forward flips then tried an equal number in the opposite direction...or that was what it felt like, anyway. Suddenly she could remember in exquisite detail the cool, firm touch of his lips, the way they'd grown warmer and more pliant when she'd persisted...

She took a deep breath but the memory wouldn't go away no matter how hard she willed it to. Why? She'd been kissed many times in the past, yet she doubted that she could have summoned up the memory of even one of those kisses even if she'd tried to. However, it was almost too easy to recall how Jack's mouth had felt—

'Are you going to stand there all day, admiring yourself, Staff? I want to leave in half an hour so I suggest you get something to eat, otherwise you'll find yourself going hungry!'

Jack had disappeared again before she'd turned around but the very air seemed to vibrate with the echo of his presence. Meg felt the tremors flow across the room and hit her squarely in the chest so that she shivered. He'd come and gone in less than three seconds but, a bit like the swell a boat made in water, she could *feel* where he'd been.

Meg's eyes were dark with sudden fear as she caught sight of herself in the mirror which, despite what he believed, she hadn't noticed before. Last night she'd wanted to stir up some sort of emotional response inside Jack, but had she given any thought to what she might be letting herself in for? By unleashing his emotions, had she given free rein to her own? Yet what did she feel? Hurt, anger, admiration, pain? All or none of those?

She sighed as she turned away from her reflection. She was

beginning to wish that she'd left Jack, his disastrous marriage *and* his feelings well alone!

'I needed that! What a morning.'

Lesley pulled over a stool and plonked her feet onto it. She and Meg had just finished their lunch, a hastily made sandwich. Meg picked up the big metal pot which seemed to be always at the ready and refilled their mugs with dark brown tea.

'Thanks!' Lesley downed half the mugful then let her head drop back with a weary sigh. 'I'm getting too old for this malarkey! This is going to be my last trip.'

'You said that last time and the time before if I remember rightly.' Rory stuffed a huge chunk of corned-beef sandwich into his mouth and swallowed it without bothering to chew it. He always ate at a rate of knots, downing his meals as though he hadn't seen food for months. But it didn't seem to trouble his digestion one iota, Meg thought, offering him her last sandwich to finish off.

'Sure you don't want it?' Rory barely paused before he wolfed it down. A full mug of tea acted as a chaser before he went to fetch the biscuit tin. Lesley exchanged an amused glance with Meg but it was obvious that she was very fond of Rory.

'I know I did. I say it every time we come on one of these jaunts, and I mean it, too. However, once I get back to civilisation, things never seem to be as bad with the advent of hindsight.' She grinned, her cheerful face full of self-mockery. 'Must have a screw loose is all I can think!'

Meg laughed softly. 'I very much doubt that. I think it would be funny if you didn't regret coming at some point or other.'

'Uh-oh, sounds like the shine is rubbing off fast for our newest recruit. Don't tell me you're already wondering why you volunteered for this when you could have been at home, enjoying yourself?'

The teasing note in Lesley's voice didn't quite hide her

concern. Meg grimaced because she hadn't realised how that might have sounded. 'Of course not. I'm really enjoying it.'

'Must be a masochist, then.' Rory popped a digestive biscuit into his mouth and swallowed it whole. 'What's up with our revered boss today? He hasn't given you a minute's peace, has he? Have you two had some sort of falling out?'

'We never had a falling *in*!' Meg declared a shade too pointedly. She saw two sets of eyebrows rise and wished she'd kept her own counsel.

'I thought you and Jack were starting to get on better,' Lesley observed quietly. 'After all, he seemed keen to have you work with him.'

'Mmm. And talking about work, I'd better see what he's got planned for this afternoon.' Meg got to her feet and took her dishes to the sink to rinse them, not wanting to be drawn into talking about Jack and the problems they seemed to have, working together.

She dried her hands on a towel then inched past Rory to get to the door. The kitchen-cum-dining area was tiny and there wasn't much room to move around. In fitting out the train, its use as a hospital had been the main consideration and everything else had been slotted in around that.

She stepped over Rory's sprawled legs and reached for the doorhandle, pausing when Lesley laughed. 'Don't tell me he's kept it a secret. Maybe he thought you'd chicken out if he gave you prior warning.'

'Prior warning about what?' Meg stopped dead as a mental traffic light switched from green to red. There was an uncomfortable fizzing in the pit of her stomach which, she realised, was a severe attack of nerves setting in. Exactly what had Jack got planned for her?

'About this little trip you two are going on?' Lesley sighed. 'Honestly, I can't believe he hasn't told you about it!'

Meg smiled but the taut curl of her lips was a travesty. 'Well, take it from me that he hasn't! So, come on…give!'

'You and Jack are going to one of the villages about ten…fifteen miles from here. Evidently, they've had a lot of cases of trachoma there and he's keen to do something about it… Are you sure he hasn't mentioned it?'

Lesley sighed even harder when Meg shook her head. 'Drat! I know he said he was going to have a word with you last night when you were outside, talking to Guy and Alison. I can't imagine why he didn't tell you then.'

Meg's smile felt as though it were riveted in place. She had a pretty good idea why Jack had overlooked telling her and she couldn't blame him for it! 'No. We…we sort of got side-tracked,' she muttered.

'Oh, well. Not to worry, eh? You'll probably enjoy it. It will give you a chance to see a bit more of the country.' Lesley collected her dishes and nudged Rory out of the way as she went to the sink. 'And you'll only be away the one night, I expect.'

'Away? You mean that Jack and I will have to stay over at this village?'

Meg's voice had risen, sounding decidedly squeaky as she tried to absorb that thought. It made Jack's voice sound all the deeper in contrast when he suddenly spoke from the corridor behind her.

'Yes. I want to instigate a hygiene routine in the village and I need time to convince the people that it's the answer to their problems.'

He shrugged when she turned to face him but she could tell that he was nowhere near as nonchalant as he tried to appear. 'We'll stay there definitely one night but it may be two, so make sure you take whatever you need with you. I take it that you don't have a problem with that, Meg?'

Then he took it wrong! Of course she had a problem, a very big one, in fact. Six feet two of problem, no less!

Meg gulped but the words couldn't be said because she wouldn't give him the satisfaction of hearing them. 'No. I don't have a problem with that,' she declared, then waited to be struck down by a thunderbolt for telling such a gigantic lie.

It didn't happen, of course. Instead, Jack treated her to a cool smile which gave her little clue as to whether or not he believed her. 'In that case, I'll see you outside in five minutes' time.'

Meg looked at her watch as he disappeared, watching the second hand ticking its way around the dial. She felt like a prisoner on death row must feel, counting off the seconds until she met her fate. She and Jack were going to spend the next twenty-four hours on their own together—how would she cope?

Thirty seconds passed and then a minute before she managed to get herself moving. Hurrying to her cabin, she dragged her holdall from under the bunk and crammed clothes into it all higgledy-piggledy. T-shirt, shorts, socks—what else would she need?

She frantically looked round the tiny compartment but she couldn't seem to think straight so in the end she just zipped the bag shut. She was standing beside the train when Jack drew the Land Rover to a halt. He leant over and thrust open the door for her.

'Throw your bag in the back,' he ordered, 'and let's get moving.'

Meg did as she was told because it was easier than arguing, but a 'please' would have been nice. She slammed the door, then clung hold of the seat as Jack set off up the steep incline. The car's wheels spun on the loose gravel, its engine whining before the tyres found a purchase.

Meg's teeth snapped together as they rocketed up the slope and surged over the top in a shower of dust, then began the equally steep descent down the other side. Jack chanced a glance at her, busily working wheel and brake as they negotiated the scree-covered escarpment.

'OK?' he shouted above the roar of the engine.

'Fine,' she shouted back, refusing to shut her eyes and give him the satisfaction of knowing how scared she was as they slithered and bounced their way down to mercifully flat ground. He didn't say anything else and she didn't attempt to break the silence as they drove to the village. Maybe it was for the best. Look what had happened the last time they'd had

a heart-to-heart. Better not to risk a repeat perfor-
mance…wasn't it?

Meg closed her eyes, not caring what he thought. It was
undoubtedly foolish but she couldn't resist letting her mind
take her back to that moment when Jack had responded to her
kiss. A small smile curved her lips. Despite everything, she
didn't regret it!

CHAPTER SIX

'THAT'S sixteen so far. How many have you seen?'

Jack looked worn out as he plonked himself down on the log Meg was sitting on. It was late afternoon and the sun was riding low in the sky. They'd worked steadily as they'd examined the villagers for signs of trachoma, and the figures weren't good.

Now Meg sighed as she glanced at her list. 'Fifteen definite and several more who look as though they could be in the early stages of the disease.'

'So that's over a third of the villagers suffering from it. Worse than I hoped but about what I expected,' Jack said flatly. 'Poor sanitation and an inadequate water supply are the two main contributing factors, and both apply here.'

They both fell silent as they looked around. Meg had been shocked by the poverty that had met them when they'd arrived at the village. It was obvious that the people who lived there were barely scratching a living and the main reason for that was a shortage of water. Crops were dying in the fields and yielding just a tiny proportion of the food the villagers needed to exist on.

'Can't something be done to help them?' she asked worriedly, pushing back her damp hair. It had been intensely hot all afternoon long and she would have given a small fortune for a cool shower, but there was no chance of that. She dug a handkerchief out of her pocket and wiped the perspiration off her face and neck then swatted at the cloud of flies which constantly plagued everyone.

'Richard has it in hand, I'm glad to say. Evidently, one of the volunteer groups believe there's fresh water just a quarter of a mile to the east of the village so they're going to bore a well. Richard has managed to beg, borrow or steal some trucks to transport the equipment out here so that they can get started.'

'That's great!' Meg couldn't hide her delight as she smiled at Jack. She saw an odd expression cross his face before he abruptly turned away. His tone was flat when he replied, making a mockery out of the actual words.

'Yes, it's wonderful news. Once they have sufficient water, life will soon improve for these people. That's why I'm so keen to get across to them at this stage how important hygiene is.'

'I see.' Meg's heart sank because she did understand, and not just about the problems the villagers were facing either. Jack had treated her with all the reserve he might have afforded a brand-new acquaintance, but they were hardly that…not after last night! It stung to realise that he could act this way but she wasn't sure why it should do so.

Would it really have been better if he'd continued in the same vein as that morning, blaming her for everything that went wrong?

Funnily enough, Meg decided that it would. At least while he was taking her to task he was showing *some* sort of emotion, whereas when he acted like this he may as well have been dead from the neck up and down!

She jumped to her feet, suddenly impatient both with Jack and herself. They should talk about what had happened, instead of trying to gloss over it the way they'd been doing all day long. Yet neither of them seemed to have the courage or the sense to make the first move.

'Well, I don't know about you, but I'm hungry. I'm going to make myself something to eat.'

Jack uncoiled his long legs and stood up. 'I'll give you a hand to set up the Primus stove. It can be a bit awkward to get it going.'

'There's no need to bother.' Meg shrugged dismissively, still smarting from the fact that the pair of them seemed incapable of sorting things out like two responsible adults. 'I'm sure I can manage, thank you.'

'Fine. You carry on, then. I'll go and have a word with Benjamin's family to let them know how he's doing.' He didn't insist when she turned down his offer, making his way instead to one of the huts and rapping on the doorframe.

Meg sighed as she went over to the Land Rover, wishing that she hadn't been so quick to refuse his help. She and Jack were never going to resolve this if one of them didn't give a little, although it would have been nice if it didn't have to be her. After all, she'd tried to apologise to him last night and look where it had got her.

Her mind did that double-quick whirl back to the previous night's events and she sighed again. It would serve no purpose harping on about how it had felt to kiss him when it was obvious how much he regretted it. He was still in love with his ex-wife and that was all that mattered at the end of the day. He wasn't interested in other women, herself in-cluded…especially not her!

The Primus stove proved to be as recalcitrant as Jack had hinted, defying all her attempts to get it working. Meg was flushed with exertion and bad temper when she glanced up to find him leaning against a tree and watching her. Pushing back her sweat-soaked hair, she glowered at him.

'If you dare say I told you so I warn you I'll…I'll…well, I'll do something *drastic*!'

His black brows rose. 'Would I dream of saying such a thing?'

'Yes! And it would give you a lot of pleasure, too!' Meg flung the box of matches onto the ground and got up. 'Oh, to hell with it. I'm not hungry now anyway!'

She wasn't sure why she felt so angry all of a sudden. Maybe it was the pressures of the day, coming on top of ev-erything else, but she knew that she was on the verge of ex-ploding if she didn't get away. She strode down the path that led away from the village, uncaring what Jack thought about her outburst. He couldn't think any worse of her anyway, she thought with a surge of grim humour. So why worry about it?

The path wound its way through a few scrubby trees before turning sharply right to skirt the base of a cliff. Meg kept on walking, wanting to work off her anger. Because it wasn't in her nature to let things upset her, it made her feel even worse. There seemed to be little danger of her getting lost so long as she stayed on the path, so she wasn't worried about that. As for any other dangers—like wild animals, for instance—she was confident that she could handle the situation if it arose. It was only Jack Trent she couldn't handle, Jack who possessed this ability to arouse in her the strangest feelings!

Meg walked for a good fifteen minutes before deciding that she should turn back. The sun was barely skimming the tree-tops now and she knew how quickly night would fall. She paused to look around, drinking in the beauty of the country-side as it lay bathed in the glow from the setting sun.

The parched landscape was golden brown and shimmering with heat, the mountains bruised purple patches against a cloudless sky. Oncamba was so beautiful but so harsh to the people who lived there. Yet, no matter what happened, Meg knew that she would always be glad that she'd come here. It had given her a new perspective on life, made her more aware of how lucky she was. If only Jack loved her then life would have been complete.

The thought slid into her mind and Meg's breath caught as she turned blindly back towards the village. There was no future in thinking like that—just a whole lot of heartache—but it was hard to rid herself of the thought. When she heard a small wailing cry she wondered for a moment if she had herself uttered it. However, when she heard it a second time, she realised that it hadn't come from her lips at all.

She stopped and looked around, trying to pinpoint where the sound was coming from. It was very quiet in the pre-dusk hour, with just the whispering of the breeze in the dry grass to disturb the silence. Even so, Meg knew that she might no have heard the noise if she hadn't been listening for it because it was so faint.

She stepped cautiously off the path and headed towards where she thought the sound had come from. The ground was treacherous beneath the cliff and she was very aware of how easy it would be to break an ankle if she didn't watch each step. She picked her way between the boulders, pausing every few seconds to listen, but she couldn't hear anything now. She was just wondering if she'd been mistaken when she spotted a bit of bright blue cloth sticking out from behind a rock.

She hurried towards it then recoiled as a dreadful smell met her. Digging in her pocket, she found a handkerchief and held it to her face as she crossed the last few yards. She was dreading what she would find, and it was as bad as she'd feared, she realised when she saw the body of an old woman lying on the ground.

There was obviously nothing she could do for the woman, but it was the glimpse of another scrap of fabric, bright red this time, that made her move closer. Her eyes widened in horror when she saw a child huddled in the rocks. It was a little girl from what she could tell, weak and dreadfully emaciated, a huge gash on her right leg surrounded by a cloud of flies.

Meg hurriedly picked her way over to the child, steeling herself as she felt for a pulse. Her heart lifted because there it was, very faint and thready but a sign all the same that she was alive!

'Meg! Where are you? Answer me!'

Jack's voice couldn't have been more welcome, though it was hard to ignore the anger it held. Meg cupped her hands to her mouth and shouted back.

'Over here! Hurry, Jack!'

He made it in double-quick time so that he was panting when he ground to a halt. He took in the situation at a glance then started firing questions at her. 'Is she alive? Has she said anything?'

'Yes, she's alive but only just. Her pulse is so faint that it took me all my time to find it. I heard her cry out, which is how I came to find her,' she explained hurriedly.

'Right. Let's get her back to the village, pronto.'

Jack didn't waste any more time. Bypassing the body of the old woman, he bent and scooped the child into his arms. She whimpered pitifully, her head lolling against his shoulder like a rag doll's. It was obvious to Meg that she wouldn't survive much longer and her heart was in her mouth as they hurried back to the village. It seemed the longest fifteen minutes of her life!

'I want saline and antibiotics, stat!' Jack bit out as he carried the child into the village. Most of the villagers were sitting outside their huts, eating their evening meals, and their arrival created a lot of interest. Meg saw Jack frown as a crowd started hurrying towards them.

'I also need some place quiet to examine her.'

Meg looked round, her gaze centring on the headman who'd come out of his hut to see what was happening. She ran over to him, using a combination of mime and words to explain what she needed. Few of the villagers spoke much English and she was afraid that he wouldn't understand her. It was a relief when he nodded and pointed to one of the huts.

She ran back to Jack. 'Over there. We can use that hut.'

'Thanks.' His eyes were warm when he smiled at her. 'Well done, Meg. I should have known you'd come up trumps.'

He carried the child to the hut, bending almost double to duck beneath the low lintel. Meg felt an inane little smile start to tilt her lips but she didn't try to stop it. A few words of praise maybe, but they meant a lot to her!

She quickly ransacked the supplies they'd brought with them, blessing Jack for his foresight when she found everything she needed. He was bending over the little girl when she went into the hut, but he looked up as soon as he heard her.

'Get that drip set up right away. Put two lines in because we need to rehydrate her as fast as possible. We'll run the antibiotics in at the same time so they can start working, but it's going to be touch and go.'

He stepped back to give her room to work and Meg gasped in horror when she suddenly got a good look at the child's injured leg. Her stomach lurched ominously as she saw the seething mass of maggots in the open wound.

'It's not as bad as you might think.' Jack squeezed her shoulder, steadying her when she needed it most. 'Those maggots will probably have saved her life by eating the rotted flesh. Once we clean up that cut you'll see what I mean.'

His pragmatism was what she needed, although she knew that the hand on her shoulder had helped as well. Meg swallowed hard and somehow managed not to make a fool of herself.

Jack gave her shoulder a last encouraging squeeze then carried on with his examination, working quickly and deftly as he tested the child's limbs for fractures. Meg followed his lead and set up the drips, one in the child's arm and the other in her uninjured leg. She was very conscious of how flaccid the child's skin felt when she cleaned it with alcohol prior to inserting the cannulae and how difficult it was to find a suitable vein. However, she managed at last and breathed a sigh of relief when the fluids started to flow into the inert little body. Step one successfully accomplished. Now for step two...the one she was dreading!

'Lucky I brought some ether with me. I was in two minds whether to or not, but it's useful on occasion.' Jack tipped a little ether onto a pad of sterile gauze and held it close to the wound on the child's leg. To Meg's amazement the maggots immediately rolled themselves up into little balls. Jack quickly began scooping them out of the way, shaking his head when Meg stepped forward to help him.

'No, leave this to me. I'm an old hand at dealing with these little squirmy things.' He grinned as he deposited the last maggot into a plastic container. 'I used to spend most weekends fishing when I was a boy. My mum always knew where to find me, down by the local pond.'

Meg laughed at the wry note in his voice but she was touched by his consideration. Despite the lightness of his tone, she knew that Jack had wanted to spare her from having to deal with the maggots when he knew how distasteful she would find it. It was an effort to keep her own tone as light as his had been as her stupid heart surged.

'I can't imagine you as a grubby-kneed little boy,' she teased, opening a fresh sachet of saline to wash out the wound.

'No? Well, I certainly wasn't a little Lord Fauntleroy, that's for sure. Thanks.' Jack swilled a little saline into the cut then grinned at her. 'I was the bane of my poor mother's life, forever getting into scrapes at school and coming home with the knees ripped out of my uniform trousers or ink blotches on my shirt. I have three older sisters and I don't think she knew what had hit her when I arrived!'

'If you were anything like my brother then I sympathise with her. David was a holy terror when he was younger. Mum used to keep a diary of all the times she and Dad were called in to see his teachers for some misdemeanour or other he'd committed.'

Meg chuckled as she reached for a kidney dish as Jack swilled the wound once more, holding it steady to catch the bloodied saline solution. 'Come birthdays and Christmas, she'd tot up how many offences David had committed and threaten him that he wouldn't get any presents unless he bucked up his ideas!'

Jack laughed at that. 'Thank heavens my mum never thought of that. I would *never* have had any presents if she'd used a point-scoring system!'

His smile lit up his whole face and for a moment Meg basked in its glow before he looked away. His tone was far more sombre when he next spoke, but that didn't mean she missed the undercurrent it held and her heart began to play pat-a-cake.

Jack had looked at her just now as he might have looked at a woman he found deeply attractive. She knew that and so did he! It was an effort to focus on what he was saying as her mind ran riot with the idea.

'You can see what I meant about those maggots, can't you?

I know how disgusting they look but they can actually be a blessing in a situation like this.'

Meg blinked as she stared at the wound on the child's leg. 'There's no sign of infection!'

She gently traced the healthy, pink tissue with a gloved finger. 'I've rarely seen a wound that clean, even one which has been treated under the strictest sterile conditions.'

'I know. Amazing, isn't it? Yet not quite such a surprise when you remember that before the discovery of antibiotics maggots were often used to clean wounds. Their use goes back thousands of years and is well documented from the time of the Ancient Egyptians right through to just after the First World War, in fact.'

Jack gave the wound one last rinse then picked up a large pad of sterile gauze. 'Soldiers who had lain on the battlefields were often found to have maggots in their wounds. However, they rarely died from secondary infections. The maggots ate away all the decaying flesh and kept the wound clean.'

'I didn't know that. I suppose I just reacted the way most people would when I saw them, but now I can see that the poor child was lucky in a way,' Meg observed gravely.

'She was. However, she isn't in the clear yet.' Jack's tone was equally grave as he finished dressing the little girl's leg. 'I'll leave it open for now as too much tissue has been lost to even think of suturing it. In other circumstances I'd be putting her down for a skin graft but we'll have to wait and see before we go making any plans.'

'She's very dehydrated. And shocked, too, I imagine.' Meg's tone was sad as she laid a gentle hand on the child's head. 'I wonder how long she'd lain there?'

'A few days, I'd say. And in this heat…well!' Jack shook his head sadly. 'Poor kid. From the look of her she wasn't in the best of health in the first place because she's certainly very emaciated. I don't hold too many hopes that she'll pull through.'

'But we'll give it our best shot!' Meg declared forcefully.

'We will. But you know that she's going to need round-the-clock nursing care if there's any hope of her recovering, don't you, Meg? And that isn't going to be easy.'

'It isn't a problem.' Meg shrugged dismissively. 'Once we get her back to the *Angel* I can sleep in the ward with her. And through the day one of us will be on hand to keep an eye on her.'

'That would be placing a lot of extra responsibility on you, Meg. You'd be on call virtually twenty-four hours a day.'

'I don't mind!' she declared passionately. 'If that's what it takes to pull her through this then I'm happy to do it.'

'Well, if you're sure it's what you want to do, I'll get things organised.' Jack's tone was pensive, as was the look he gave her, but Meg wasn't sure *what* he was thinking.

She managed a smile, struggling to keep all trace of anything untoward from her face. To let Jack know how desperately she wanted him to be thinking *good* things about her could be setting herself up for a great deal of disappointment.

'I am sure. And I know that Lesley and Kate will back me up.'

'Right, then I'd better go and see if anyone knows who she is. Obviously, we'll need to get her parents' permission to treat her but, hopefully, that won't be a problem.' Jack treated her to a quick but surprisingly warm smile before he left the hut.

Meg turned back to their small patient and set about washing the child's pitifully thin body. It was a task that demanded little concentration because she'd performed it hundreds of times before. However, she kept her mind firmly on what she was doing. She'd allowed herself far too much leeway already that day to risk letting her thoughts go wandering where they chose again.

The night was very dark now that the moon was hidden behind a cloud for once. Meg sat on a box of medical supplies while she listened to the chirping of the crickets. Behind her in the hut the little girl slept peacefully. They still had no idea who she was because she wasn't from the village. However, there had been a slight but encouraging improvement in her con dition as the drips had started to put back the lost fluids into her body.

Meg was hopeful that she would pull through but it was still very much at the fingers-crossed stage. It could go either way but if a few heartfelt prayers and a large dollop of will-power had anything to do with it, the child would recover.

Closing her eyes, she rested her head against the rough wattle wall of the hut. The heat was beginning to catch up with her now and she felt physically drained. She was almost asleep when something alerted her to the fact that she was being watched.

Her heavy lids drifted open and she stared at Jack for a moment before she managed to summon a rueful smile. 'I wasn't really asleep. I was just resting my eyes.'

'Mmm, you tell a good tale, Staff Nurse Andrews.' He grinned back at her as he dragged over another packing case and sat down. Leaning against the wall, he stretched out his long legs with a sigh. 'I'm bushed and I don't mind admitting it.'

'So am I, to be honest. I just didn't want to be the first to admit it in case you saw it as a sign of weakness.' Meg grinned sleepily at him and saw him frown.

'There's no shame in admitting that you're tired, Meg. Working in this heat is bad enough, but when you combine it with the sort of gruelling schedule we have… Well!'

He half turned to look at her. 'You aren't forgetting to take care of yourself, I hope? It's easy to get so caught up in the job that you forget about your own health. You need to make sure that you drink plenty and keep up your sodium levels and take your antimalarial tablets. And you must be on the lookout for any cuts or grazes…'

She held up her hand. 'Whoa! Steady on, Dr Trent. You'll make me so neurotic about the dangers that I won't be able to function!' She laughed when he grimaced ruefully. 'But to set your mind at rest, yes, I've done all of those things. I don't intend to let myself get ill and add to your woes if I can help it.'

'Good. But not because I'm worried about ending up with another patient. I...I wouldn't like to think of you being ill, Meg.'

His voice grated just a little but it was enough to set her pulse off and running. Meg stared down at her hands, studying her nails as though they were the most fascinating sight she'd seen in her life. This could go any of several ways and she wasn't sure which direction to choose until Jack suddenly took charge of the situation.

Her eyes were as big as saucers as he took hold of her hand and gave her a gentle tug that tipped her towards him. They grew even wider when she saw his mouth tilt into the sexiest, most provocative smile she'd ever seen! Maybe that was what made her come out with the most inane statement of her life, one which made her squirm with mortification the moment she'd uttered it.

'Wh-what are you doing?'

'What do you think?' His breath was warm on her mouth as he bent towards her.

'Do...do you think it's a good idea?' she whispered, almost groaning out loud at her tongue's perversity. *She* didn't want to argue! *She* wanted him to kiss her! So what was going on?

'Probably not. But let's live dangerously, shall we?'

His lips touched hers, skated across their surface, then moved away. Meg opened her eyes, not sure when she had actually closed them. The kiss had been too brief for conscious thought so unconsciously she must have reacted to it.

She bit her lip as she saw the heat simmering in Jack's eyes and knew what it meant. He wanted to kiss her again—a *real* kiss this time, not that teasing taster which had left her aching for more. But was it wise to let this happen when she wasn't sure why he'd kissed her in the first place?

'Too dangerous for you, Meg? Afraid that you'll regret it in the morning?' He shook his head so that a lock of crisp black hair fell onto his forehead. 'That doesn't seem like you. Last night I'd have said very little would scare you.'

'That was last night and it was different then,' she muttered.

'Different…how? You kissed me then, granted, but it was just as…*effective*.' His smile was gentle, relaxed and at ease, yet it was so out of character for him to behave this way that she couldn't accept it at face value.

'Yes, I kissed you, but I soon realised that all my good intentions had been completely misconstrued!'

'Good intentions? Mmm, that sounds ominous. Here was I thinking that you'd been overcome with desire, and all the time it was your *good* intentions which had prompted you to do it.'

There was a slight grate to his voice and a tiny flaring of his nostrils which hinted at the fact that the idea didn't please him, and she hid a smile. What a typically male reaction! It was all very well if he'd kissed her as some sort of punishment but something else entirely that she might have had another agenda than the one he'd assumed.

'That's the sort of caring person I am, though, Jack.' She shrugged, rather enjoying the fact that she could pay him back just a little for all he'd put her through. 'Seeing you like that made me want to do something to shake you out of it.'

'Like what? What was I like?' He sat back and folded his arms, his body language telling her that he wasn't pleased by her revelations. Meg experienced a momentary qualm but all day long she'd wanted to get this out into the open and talk about it. Now was her chance to do exactly that.

'All turned in on yourself, of course. All your emotions buttoned up and locked away. You can't live like that, Jack. It isn't right.' She turned to him beseechingly. 'You have to let yourself *feel* otherwise you aren't really alive!'

He gave a short, harsh laugh which made her flinch because she could hear the pain it contained. 'I tried that, thank you. I felt every emotion under the sun when I was married to Briony and I think I'll pass on that sort of experience again. I try not to repeat my worst mistakes.'

He stood up abruptly but Meg leapt to her feet as well, plonking herself directly in his path when he tried to walk away. 'That's a coward's way out, Jack Trent!'

'So what if it is? At least it means that I can direct all my energy towards things that matter. Love takes a toll on you, Meg, if you haven't found that out for yourself. It saps your will to get on with your life.'

It was such a stark idea that she felt her eyes fill with tears. 'That isn't true! OK, so you've had one bad experience but that doesn't mean you shouldn't try again. It's like…like falling off a horse and refusing to get back on in case it happens a second time!'

'Mmm, probably a bit more painful than that, although I appreciate what you're trying to say. It's just a pity that I have no intention of taking your well-meaning advice. Love isn't for me, Meg. I've had all I want or need of it to last me a couple of lifetimes.'

Meg couldn't stop the tears from flowing then. She knew she was making a fool of herself but she couldn't help it. She heard Jack mutter something as he drew her into his arms but she wasn't sure what he'd said.

'Don't cry, Meg. It's not worth crying about, believe me. It's over and done with and that's the end of it.' His tone was rough yet strangely gentle at the same time, and somehow it made her cry all the harder. She heard him sigh as he held her closer. 'Shh, now. Don't be silly.'

'It's…not…silly,' she gulped between sobs. 'It's…it's… Oh, I don't know what it is!'

She tipped her head back so that she could glare at him and saw his eyes darken as he took stock of her tear-streaked face. A look of indecision crossed his face before he suddenly bent and his lips were so tender when they found hers that Meg's heart seemed to stop.

He gave a husky murmur, although whether from pleasure or regret she wasn't sure, before he suddenly deepened the kiss and she was lost. The whole world seemed to tilt on its axis when she felt the burning assault of Jack's mouth as he kissed her with every scrap of emotion he'd held back before.

Meg's head was reeling from the aftershocks as wave after wave of emotion flooded through her. Every single huma emotion seemed to be encompassed in the kiss—from passion to hatred, from anger to desire. Yet slowly they all receded like a high tide after a storm until there was only one left, perhaps the most precious of all. To have Jack kiss her as though he cared for her was the most shocking, the most sensual, the most wonderful feeling of all!

He let her go, slowly, reluctantly yet with deliberation. In the pale, hazy moonlight his face was just a shadow. Meg could feel her heart drumming inside her and knew that he could feel it as well. Maybe his was making the same sort of racket but she couldn't seem to focus on anything other than her own feelings at that moment.

Jack brushed her mouth with his knuckles in the lightest of caresses, yet she almost cried out at the sensations it aroused in her. 'If I was going to let myself fall in love again then I think it would be with someone like you, Meg.'

Her eyes blurred but she wouldn't cry, not again. 'Thank you…I think!'

It was such a pitiful attempt at humour but Jack smiled all the same. Maybe he sensed how much it had cost her and was grateful that she'd made the effort and hadn't made a scene. 'You're welcome. Now I think it's time we got some sleep, don't you? We have a busy day ahead of us tomorrow.'

She almost broke down at that point—almost, but not quite. Any dreams she might have harboured as a result of that kiss hadn't had time to settle in her mind, she assured herself. They were still at the *what if* stage, the hazy *wouldn't it be nice* level, and that wasn't enough to start making plans on. Yet even knowing that, it didn't make it easy to dismiss what had happened. It took an awful lot of courage, plus a big dollop of pride, to feign indifference.

'We certainly do. I'll see you in the morning, then, Jack. Sweet dreams.'

The last bit came out before she could stop it and she saw him stiffen before he walked over to the Land Rover where he would be spending the night. Meg had opted to sleep in the hut to be near the little girl and she was glad that she had.

She doubted that she was going to sleep much after what had happened, so it would be good to have something to occupy her mind.

The idea that Jack could—maybe, possibly—have loved her if the circumstances had been different was going to take a lot of getting used to!

CHAPTER SEVEN

THE little girl's name was Katu and she was an orphan now that the grandmother who had cared for her had died. Meg listened sadly as Ben Lister, a volunteer who'd been working in the area for several months, explained the child's background to them the following morning. He was one of the group who would be in charge of sinking the bore hole and he'd recognised the little girl as soon as he'd seen her.

'She and her grandmother lived in the next village. I'd heard that the old lady had taken the child to visit some of her relatives.' Ben took off his spectacles and cleaned them abstractedly on the tail of his shirt. He had just finished university and was doing overseas aid work in a gap year before finding a job.

'The old lady knew that she wouldn't be around much longer, I imagine, and wanted one of her relations to take care of her granddaughter, but it looks as though they must have refused. You can't blame them, really. Having another mouth to feed when you're barely getting by isn't something anyone would willingly opt to do.'

'Well, at least it means that we won't have to get anyone's permission to treat her.' Jack sighed as he looked at the child. 'Not had much of a start in life, has she?'

Meg heard the sadness in his voice and hurried to cheer him up, wondering why she felt this need to comfort him all the time. Surprisingly enough, she'd passed a relatively peaceful night and hadn't lain awake, worrying about what had happened.

Apart from getting up several times to check on Katu, her sleep had been uninterrupted by any soul-searching. Jack had kissed her, told her that if he'd been in the market for another love affair then she would have been top of the list, and she had slept the sleep of the just. There simply wasn't any accounting for the way her mind worked, it seemed!

'Maybe her luck is going to change from now on. After all, she must have someone on her side to have survived such an ordeal.'

Jack smiled thinly but there were dark circles under his eyes which told their own tale about the kind of night he'd had. 'Ever the optimist, Meg?'

'Better than being a pessimist, though,' she shot back, inwardly groaning as she wondered if they were going to have round two that morning. Was she going to be made the scapegoat every time Jack *gave* a little and showed he was human? No way!

She treated him to her most chilly smile. 'Right, I'm going to give Katu a bed-bath then I'll be ready to help you. Is that OK?'

'Dare I object?' His grey eyes sparkled with sudden laughter and Meg relented. She smiled back at him with a lot more warmth and saw the flicker of emotion that crossed his face before he abruptly turned away with the muttered proviso that he wanted to get the show on the road in the next half-hour so she'd better hurry up.

Meg sighed as he and Ben went to round up the villagers. One step forward and half a step back. It was definitely slow progress, building up a relationship with Jack Trent! Maybe she should concentrate on making sure that his professional opinion of her stayed on the plus side and forget about anything personal.

That idea lasted as long as it took her to collect a bowl and pour some bottled water into it. Foolish or not, but she wanted Jack to think well of her in *every* way, although what she was hoping to achieve she wasn't sure. Still, she would worry about that if and when the time came to make it necessary.

Katu was awake but obviously still very traumatised by her ordeal. She made no murmur when Meg gently washed her thin little body but her black eyes were enormous as they followed Meg around the hut.

Meg had no idea if the little girl could understand her. Some of the older Oncamban people had learned English at the mission schools which had been run by various Christian denominations in the past. They had been shut down during the previous ruler's reign when the country had been off limits to foreigners.

The schools were gradually being set up again but whether Katu had been able to attend any of them was open to question. However, Meg didn't let that deter her as she chatted away. Maybe the child couldn't understand what she was saying but the tone of her voice would at least make it clear that there was no need for her to be frightened.

'Now, I'm just going to check how your leg is doing,' Meg explained, smiling at the little girl. 'It won't hurt, I promise.'

She gently peeled the dressing off the wound and was delighted to see how healthy the exposed tissue looked. Jack had been right to say that it would need a skin graft to heal completely, but that was something they would be able to consider once the little girl was stronger.

Ripping open a fresh packet of dressings, Meg re-dressed the wound. Katu solemnly watched what she was doing then held out her hand when Meg went to throw away the packaging in which the dressing had been wrapped.

'Do you want this, sweetheart?' Meg smiled as she handed the crackly paper to the child and watched her eyes light up. Katu crumpled the empty packet in her hand then smiled delightedly when it sprang back to its original shape the moment she released it.

Meg ran her hand over the little girl's tight black curls and sighed softly. How many children would be fascinated by a bit of paper? she wondered. It just seemed to emphasise what a huge rift there was between the children in her world and the Oncamban children.

Katu was well enough to sip a little bottled water and some of the high-protein drink Meg had mixed for her. The child's lips were so cracked and sore that Meg had to give her a straw to use, and once again Katu was fascinated by something she'd never seen before. Consequently, it all took some time, but when Meg went to find Jack she was feeling far more confident that the little girl would recover eventually.

'How is she?' Jack looked up when he heard her approaching. His face was in full sun and it was even more obvious how drawn he looked. There were deep lines grooved on either side of his mouth and knitting his brows. Meg felt suddenly impatient with him.

All right, so maybe he did regret kissing her last night and probably regretted opening up even more, but it wasn't the crime of the century, for heaven's sake! Yet he seemed intent on giving himself a hard time just because he was *human*!

'Meg? Nothing's happened, has it?' He straightened abruptly, a look of concern crossing his face as he stared towards Katu's hut. 'She is all right?'

'Yes, she's fine. I've just given her something to eat.' She sighed wearily, realising that Jack had misinterpreted her scowl. Suddenly she couldn't face another day of pussy-footing around the issue which was uppermost on both their minds.

'Look, Jack, about last night…' she began but got no further before the sound of engines suddenly disturbed the peace and quiet. They both turned to see what was happening then Jack's face suddenly broke into a huge smile.

'Richard!'

Leaving Meg standing there, he strode over to greet the tall, handsome black man who jumped down from the cab of the lead truck. He was followed by half a dozen armed guards who quickly surrounded him, but he waved them back as he stepped forward to shake Jack's hand. They spoke together for a couple of minutes before Jack brought the newcomer to meet Meg.

'Meg, this is Richard whom I've been telling you about. He's the reason why we happen to be here!'

'I only made the request for help. You are the one who got

things moving, Jack,' Richard declared. He held out his hand, his face breaking into a warm smile. 'I'm delighted to meet you, Meg. I want you to know how grateful I am to you and the rest of the people who have spared the time to come to my country and help us.'

'It's a pleasure,' Meg replied sincerely, taking an immediate liking to him. He was as tall as Jack was, with gleaming black skin and a wonderful smile. He was dressed for work in no-nonsense chinos and a bush shirt, and couldn't have looked less like her idea of the man in charge of the whole country. It was obvious that Richard preferred a hands-on approach, she decided bemusedly as he graciously excused himself and set about supervising the unloading of the machinery that would be used to dig the bore hole.

There was no time to return to their previous conversation as people were starting to arrive for their clinic by then, so Meg decided to put it on hold until later. They divided up the patients, with Jack taking the more serious cases so that he could assess who would benefit from surgery.

Meg dispensed tetracycline ointment and advice, explaining repeatedly how important it was that hands and faces were washed to avoid cross-contamination within families. Ben Lister proved himself to be a great help by interpreting for those villagers who had trouble understanding them.

After they had seen all the people actually suffering from trachoma, Jack gathered the whole village together and went through the hygiene routine one more time. Every household had been asked to provide an old tin or plastic container with a small hole bored in it. When water was poured into the leaky tin, the trickle that emerged was sufficient to wash the hands and face with, as he demonstrated to everyone's amusement. With water being so scarce, that was the biggest problem and this method, simple though it was, created very little wastage.

Meg was fascinated by it all and said so when Jack had finished. 'How did you think up that idea? It's brilliant!'

'I can't take credit for it, I'm afraid. I read about some trials that have been carried out with the Masai and took it from that. Evidently, it's been extremely successful in cutting the number of cases of trachoma that occur within their community. Obviously, it needs follow-up care—someone to administer the antibiotics and keep a check, and so on—but that won't be a problem here because Ben has volunteered to do it,' he explained.

'And once the villagers see the results for themselves, they will be all the keener to continue the routine?' Meg said thoughtfully.

'Exactly. Not to mention that the situation will ease a lot once that bore hole has been dug. When you live in England, you don't realise just how precious water is!' he added ruefully, making her laugh.

'Mmm, I'll remember that the next time we have an *English* summer!'

'Count your blessings, Meg,' Jack said lightly, gathering up his equipment to pack it away.

'I will if you will.' She wished she hadn't said that, but it was impossible to take it back. Jack's brows winged upwards.

'Meaning?' he asked silkily, but with just enough inflection to put her off if she'd let it. She didn't! He could come the *Dr* Jack Trent act if he chose to, but she wasn't going to be deterred from saying her piece even though she knew she was probably wasting her breath.

'*Meaning* that you have a lot to be thankful for, just as I do, Jack. You have your health and a job you love. You have friends who care about you and people who admire what you stand for. Put all those in the plus column and they'll certainly outweigh the minuses.'

She didn't mention the *big* minus, of course—his failed marriage. However, she knew that he'd probably filled it in His smile was just a little too forced to be genuine.

'I'll bear it in mind, Meg. Now, I think it's about time we returned to the *Angel*, don't you?'

One last smile and he was gone. Meg sighed as she went to get Katu ready for the journey. She had a feeling that Jack thought she was an interfering busybody! Still, why let that bother her? It could have been worse…couldn't it?

The others were gratifyingly pleased to have them back on board the train. Meg suspected that it was more the delight at having two more pairs of hands to share the workload than the fact they'd been missed! However, as she'd predicted, both Lesley and Kate immediately offered to share the extra burden of looking after Katu with her. They brushed aside her assurances that she didn't expect it, and set up a rota. One of them would sleep in the hospital carriage each night to be on hand if the little girl needed anything.

Transporting Katu back to the *Angel* had been easier than they'd feared because Richard had offered to let them use one of his trucks. They were able to make the child fairly comfortable in the back and Meg had travelled with her. Jack had wanted to do it but as she couldn't drive the Land Rover he'd had to accept that it was the only way.

Richard had waved them off after promising to catch up with them at a later date. He'd asked after the rest of the team and had shown concern when he'd learned that Yvonne Fleming hadn't been well enough to accompany them. Meg hadn't realised that Richard knew the nurse who she'd replaced and mentioned it to Lesley while they were waiting for their turn in the tiny bathroom that night.

Lesley sighed as she pulled a ragged lump off her sponge and tossed it out of the open carriage door. 'I'm not sure what the situation is there but I have my suspicions. I thought it odd when Yvonne backed out at the last minute, to tell the truth. I suspect it had more to do with the thought of meeting up with Richard again than the fact that she wasn't well enough to make this trip.'

'So they know one another well, do they?' Meg queried.

'*Very* well, from what I can gather. Richard lived in England from when he was quite young. His family were expelled from Oncamba by the previous ruler. One of the reasons why he's so down-to-earth is because he and his family didn't have it easy—they had to leave everything behind when they fled the country and arrived in England with virtually nothing. Anyway, Richard and Yvonne were at university together, I believe, and very close at one time.'

'I see. So you think Yvonne felt awkward about running into him again if they'd once had a relationship and split up?'

'Something like that. Relationships are always difficult and a mixed-race one must create its own problems even in this day and age.' Lesley looked round as the bathroom door opened and Rory appeared. 'And about time, too. Who says that it takes a woman longer to get ready than a man? Obviously, they've not shared a bathroom with you, Rory O'Donnell!'

'Is it my fault that I need extra time to make myself presentable?' Rory looked soulfully at them. 'Just because you two are natural visions of loveliness and don't need to resort to all the primping and preening it takes to make me look halfway human!' He sighed sadly. 'Have you no compassion in your heart for the afflicted, Lesley?'

'Not if it means you hogging all the hot water, no!' Lesley whisked through the door then paused to smile sweetly at Rory. 'Anyway, I'm sure Jack will appreciate all the trouble you've taken to make yourself presentable for his birthday party, so don't feel too downhearted.'

'Birthday party? It's Jack's birthday today, you mean?' Meg couldn't hide her surprise.

'Yes. Didn't he mention it?' Lesley rolled her eyes. 'I expect he's forgotten all about it, knowing him. It's a good job that some of us are on the ball and have got things organised. We're throwing a party for him tonight so make sure you put on your best bib and tucker!'

Meg shook her head in bemusement as Lesley slammed the bathroom door. 'I had no idea. I wish he'd mentioned it.'

'Probably didn't think you'd be interested. Or didn't want you to know how old he is.' Rory grinned. 'If I was thirty-seven, I'd be keeping quiet about it, too!'

Meg laughed as he strolled unhurriedly back to his compartment. Rory had an answer for everything!

She frowned. Had Jack forgotten it was his birthday or had he chosen not to mention it to her? She had no real idea so it would be foolish to decide it was the latter. However, she couldn't help wondering if, by not telling her, he'd been trying to keep a little more distance between them. It was hard to dismiss that thought and it hurt just a little and definitely more than it should!

'A toast, folks. To Jack—may he keep on running these holiday trips for many years to come!'

Everyone laughed at Rory's droll toast. Meg shook her head as she put down her glass of wine. 'Holiday trips, indeed!'

Alison, seated beside her, laughed. 'Not quite a week in Bognor Regis, is it? Still, I bet you're glad you came, aren't you?'

Meg smiled, her eyes going instinctively to where Jack sat at the opposite end of the table, squashed into what had been laughingly declared the seat of honour. 'Yes,' she replied softly, knowing that it was true. 'Yes, I'm glad I came.'

Jack suddenly looked up and his eyes met hers along the length of the table. Meg felt her heart begin to race when she saw the awareness they held. Suddenly it felt as though all the noise and laughter had faded into the background as they looked at one another. There was a fizzing in her veins, a humming in her head, a feeling of expectancy coursing through her, before Alison elbowed her sharply in the ribs and everything returned to normal once more.

'Hey, are you OK? You looked as though you'd gone into a trance.' The girl shot a look down the table then gave a knowing smile. 'Oh, I see. That's how the wind blows, is it?'

Guy claimed her attention just then and Meg breathed a sigh of relief at having been spared the need to answer. Frankly, she wasn't sure what she would have said. Maybe the wind was *blowing*, as Alison had so eloquently put it, but she wasn't sure in which direction!

Jack rapped on the table with the handle of his knife to claim their attention, and she fixed her gaze on a spot a little to the left of his head, deeming it safer. No more lingering looks until she was sure what they meant, she decided, then almost laughed out loud at the stupidity of that thought. When had she ever known the true state of play since she'd met Jack Trent?

'I won't bore you by making a speech, folks—' he began.

'Then you'll be the first doctor I've ever met who's passed up the chance,' Kate declared pithily, making everyone chuckle.

'Thank you, Kate. I shall keep it even shorter, then.' Jack grinned at her before he looked round the table. 'Anyway, I just wanted to thank you all for tonight. I'd completely forgotten it was my birthday, to tell the truth, so it came as a double surprise. I appreciate it.'

Everyone clapped before Rory got up to refill their glasses. Meg put her hand over her glass to signal that she didn't want any more wine. She shook her head when Rory frowned. 'No, honestly. I don't have much of a head for drink. Another glass and I won't be responsible for my actions!'

Rory leered comically at her. 'Sounds great to me!'

Meg laughed at his teasing. It was impossible to take offence because there wasn't a nasty bone in Rory's body. It was odd, then, that when she happened to glance up she saw the angry look Jack gave the younger man.

Meg looked away but her heart was hammering faster than it should have been. Had Jack been annoyed because he'd thought that Rory was giving her a come-on? She tried to dismiss the idea by joining in the conversation as it flowed around the table, but it stayed at the back of her mind—niggling, tantalising, tormenting. It was a relief when she happened to glance at her watch and realised that it was time to check on Katu because it meant that she had a legitimate excuse to make her escape.

Squeezing out of her seat, Meg edged past the others, grinning when Kate ruefully muttered something about wishing she hadn't eaten so much when she tried to pull her chair closer to the table to let her pass. Jack was right next to the door and he got up to move his chair out of the way so that she could open it.

'Thanks.' Meg avoided looking directly at him as she slid out of the door and hurried along the corridor. Her nerves were a little too tightly strung to have risked making eye contact. How would Jack feel if he knew that she'd sussed him out, realised that he'd been *jealous* when Rory had passed that remark? Probably about as stunned as she'd felt!

Katu was awake when Meg went into the hospital carriage. There were just four beds in there, each one sited next to a bank of monitoring equipment. Meg found herself wondering what the little girl thought of being surrounded by all the high-tech machinery.

It must seem like a whole different world to her, a world that was both unfamiliar and scary. However, there didn't appear to be any sign of fear on the child's face when Meg approached her bed. Far from it, in fact, as she saw Katu give her a shy smile. The child's unconditional trust touched her deeply and she swore to herself that, no matter how difficult it was going to be, she would make sure that this child was taken care of for the rest of her life.

'Hello, darling. How are you?' She smiled at the little girl as she took her pulse. It was a lot stronger than it had been, its beat even and steady, and she nodded. 'That's very good, poppet. Now, let me take your temperature.'

Taking the thermometer from its holder, she slid it under the child's armpit and waited a few seconds before checking the reading. Once again she was pleasantly surprised when she found that Katu's temperature was almost normal.

'What a clever little girl you are!' Meg declared, popping the thermometer back into its holder and noting down the reading on the chart. She hung it back on the end of the bed then checked the drip, turning it down a fraction. Hopefully, they would be able to take Katu off the drip in a day or so as by then she should be taking enough fluids orally not to need it.

She'd been lucky and once the wound on her leg had been dealt with she should recover, although what would happen to her in the future was something Meg would need to find out.

'Right, that's great,' she declared, straightening the sheet and plumping up the pillows. Katu continued to watch her with huge, solemn eyes, showing no sign of wanting to go to sleep. Meg pulled over a chair and sat beside the bed, loath to leave the little girl there on her own.

'Not sleepy yet? How about if I tell you a story?'

The child smiled, although Meg doubted whether she'd understood. She didn't let it deter her, however, settling back in the chair as she began with the well-worn line with which all the best fairy-stories began. 'Once upon a time there was a beautiful princess and her name was Katu.'

The child's face lit up when she recognised her own name. Snuggling down against the pillows, she appeared to listen intently as Meg carried on. It was very quiet in the carriage because they were well away from where the others were partying. Meg lowered her voice, speaking softly as she wove her tale about a beautiful princess who met her handsome prince in the forest one day. It seemed the most natural thing in the world to name the prince Jack so she didn't pause to give it any thought.

Katu's lids were drooping as Meg neared the end of her story. The little girl gave a massive yawn then closed her eyes with a sigh of contentment. Meg smiled as she quietly stood up.

'And the beautiful princess and handsome Prince Jack lived happily ever after,' she whispered, turning to creep away. It was only then that she realised that she'd added an extra listener to her audience. Heat swept up her face when she saw Jack leaning against the doorjamb. It took her all her time to walk towards him, but where else could she have gone? There was one way in and one way out, and the fact that he was standing slap bang in the centre of it meant that she had to pass him!

He waited until she was almost facing him before he spoke,

and she heard the bemusement in his voice with a sinking heart.

'Prince *Jack*?'

Meg came to a halt and shrugged. 'Why not? It…it was the first name that came to mind, that's all.'

'I see. So it wasn't that you used *me* as your role model? Pity. I rather liked that idea.'

Meg stared at him, wondering if she'd heard right. Jack was teasing her about making free with his name? Surely not!

She took a quick step forward then stopped when he didn't move out of her way. 'Excuse me,' she said politely, glancing pointedly at the doorway.

'Sorry. Where are my manners?' He stepped aside with a lavish bow, his grey eyes glinting wickedly as he glanced up at her from his position bent double. 'Hardly what you'd expect from a prince, is it?'

Meg's mouth pursed because she wasn't sure it would be wise to let any words escape. The situation seemed to be fraught with danger, though she wasn't sure why. Jack was just having a bit of fun, teasing her about adopting his name for her fairy-story hero, so why didn't she take it in good part as he expected her to do? She wasn't sure but, then, she hadn't been sure about anything recently so it was hardly a surprise.

That was another annoying—disturbing, dangerous-seeming—thought. Meg swept past him with regal disdain, refusing to sully her mind with any more such unsavoury thoughts. If she could have washed it clean of Jack Trent and the effect he had on her then she would happily have done so at that moment!

Jack chuckled, or that was what it sounded like before he hurriedly cleared his throat. Meg shot him a baleful look over her shoulder as she swept along the corridor. 'What? Obviously something has amused you so out with it.'

'Me amused? Surely that's a contradiction in terms? I mean, 'm the guy who doesn't feel what others feel, the one who's devoid of human emotions.'

Her lips quirked despite herself but she forced them bac
into shape. 'Well, you said it.'

'I'm not the only one, though, am I?' They'd reached he
compartment by then, and she stopped when she found an arr
suddenly barring her way. 'That's what you accused me o
Meg. Maybe I'm beginning to think that you could be righ
And *maybe* I want to do something about it, only I'm not sur
how.'

'Only maybe?' She took a quick breath yet still felt breath
less when she saw the uncertainty in his eyes. To see Jac
looking so unsure immediately aroused the tenderest of fee
ings inside her. She wanted to reassure and comfort him
promise him that he wouldn't get hurt again, but she didn
have that kind of power. The only one who would be able t
heal his injured heart was Briony, the one who'd broken it i
the first place, the one he still loved. How it hurt to realis
that!

Her voice was flat because she was so afraid that he woul
hear the pain if she didn't erase it totally. 'You have to be on
hundred per cent sure of what you want, Jack. You need t
be committed and determined and…and…a lot of things yo
aren't now! Otherwise it won't work.'

He nodded gravely. 'So that's your advice, is it? That
make a decision and go for it?'

'Yes,' she whispered miserably, feeling for the doorhandl
'You can't be half-hearted about getting what you want from
life, Jack. You have to put as much effort into it as you pu
into your work.'

He let his arm drop and there was a rueful expression o
his handsome face. 'The trouble is that I can pretty accuratel
weigh up the odds where work is concerned, but it isn't s
easy in other areas of your life, is it? That's the worrying part

'If you're saying that there aren't any guarantees, you'r
right.' She shrugged and the small movement was almost to
much for her, sapping the last of her strength. 'You have t
take a few risks, but it would be worth it. If Briony knew ho

much you regretted getting divorced, it might help her get her own life straight.'

'Briony?' Jack's brows peaked. He suddenly laughed as he leant forward and kissed the tip of Meg's nose. 'What has Briony got to do with this? My ex-wife isn't part of this equation. I have no idea why you should have imagined that she had.'

Meg's mouth fell open as he calmly carried on along the corridor. She heard a burst of laughter when the lounge door opened then it was abruptly cut off as the door was closed once more. The silence came back but it was such a *noisy* silence that Meg pressed her hands over her ears. Maybe the questions were only inside her head but it felt as though they were being shouted at her. Her ears were ringing from the assault.

What had Jack meant? If he hadn't been speaking about his ex-wife then to whom had he been referring? Her, Meg Andrews? Someone else? No one in particular? Just a general observation?

Meg rushed into her compartment and slammed the door. Flinging herself on her bunk, she tried to sort through the jumble and make sense of it. She was usually good at that sort of thing but tonight she failed miserably. If Jack was thinking about getting his personal life back on track, she had no idea why!

CHAPTER EIGHT

'This is going to need a skin flap, not just a graft. Too much tissue has been lost for a graft to take. However, that kind of surgery is too delicate for us to undertake on a trip like this.'

Jack treated Katu to a warm smile as he drew the sheet over her. He felt in his pocket and produced a bright red Biro. He laughed when the little girl's eyes lit up as she eagerly reached for it. Katu adored drawing and was never happier than when she had some paper and a pen in her hands.

Meg handed the little girl the pad she'd found tucked away in the supply cupboard and left her to start on another of her pictures. The hospital bay was beginning to resemble an art gallery with Katu's pictures taped to all the walls. She'd been on board almost a week now and they'd travelled some distance from the area where she'd been found. However, the child didn't seem at all upset about the change in her circumstances, happily coping with every new development with a quiet acceptance that Meg envied.

If only *she* could cope so happily with all the turmoil which seemed to have occurred in her life of late, she would feel a lot happier!

Now she concentrated fiercely on what Jack had said because she knew how quickly her mind could start wandering if it was given the chance. Ever since the night she'd told Katu that fairy-story she'd felt as though she were on an emotional roller-coaster. The fact that Jack had never again mentioned the conversation they'd had about him getting to grips with his personal life only added to her confusion. Frankly, she didn't know what was going on but she'd be damned if she'd let him know that!

'If we can't treat her here she'll need to be transferred to a hospital.' She frowned as she considered that idea. 'It won't be in Oncamba, though, will it?'

'No. The few hospitals there are in the country simply aren't geared up for this kind of operation.' Jack tapped his teeth with a square-cut fingernail while he pondered the problem. 'I could find out if they'd admit her to a hospital in Johannesburg, but what I'd really like to do is have her sent back to England.'

'England?' Meg couldn't hide her surprise.

'Uh-huh. The best man for a job like this is Patrick Wilde. He's a real artist when it comes to this type of surgery. If I could get in contact with him I'm sure he'd agree to take Katu as a patient.'

'But wouldn't there be problems with immigration and other red tape?' she suggested.

'Not so long as we can assure the relevant authorities that the child will be returning home after treatment.' Jack smiled. 'I've done this before and usually there's someone who will bend the rules just a little!'

He held his finger and thumb a tiny way apart to show how little it needed and Meg laughed. 'Then go for it! It's in Katu's best interests after all. But what about the costs involved? It costs a fortune for an air ambulance and then the operation will need to be done privately, not on the NHS.'

'Oh, leave that to me. Patrick will undoubtedly waive his fees and we can work round the rest of the costs involved. As for getting her back to England, I'm sure I can come up with something.' Jack glanced back at the bed and his face softened when he looked at the child. 'It just needs a bit of working out and then I'm sure we'll find a solution.'

Maybe he could find one for her dilemma while he was at it, Meg thought wryly as she went back to admire the picture Katu had drawn. He seemed a master at working out problems so it should be simple for him to solve hers, although that was supposing she decided *exactly* what the problem was, of course.

Jack seemed to have accepted her as a member of his team

and that was one blessing. It was whether she wanted him to
see her as a *woman* as well as a colleague which was the real
thorny issue. Part of her did and part of her didn't because
she was afraid of what she might be letting herself in for. She
was attracted to him, liked him and had certainly enjoyed kissing him. Those were the pros but the cons were equally relevant.

He seemed to like her and was attracted to her as well. It
was also obvious that kissing her hadn't been exactly a chore.
But would he ever get over his ex-wife? He'd seemed to imply
that he could the other night but since then he'd not said a
word on the subject, which left her…where? Rudderless.
Drifting. Mixed up.

Meg sighed as she left Katu to her drawing and went to set
up for that day's surgery. Life had been so simple before she'd
met Jack Trent!

It was just on lunchtime when Lesley came hurrying into the
consulting room after a perfunctory knock on the door. 'Jack,
can you come, please?'

He didn't waste time asking questions as he turned to Meg.
'Can you carry on here, please?'

'Of course.' She watched him hurry after Lesley, wondering
what was wrong. But she would find out in all good time, she
assumed, so she turned to their patient with a reassuring smile.

Apart from the problem of trachoma, one of the other main
areas they were focusing on was the worrying number of cases
of cervical cancer amongst Oncamban women. It was a huge
problem throughout many developing countries, accounting
for numerous deaths. Jack and Guy were treating it as a major
issue on this trip.

Part of their brief was to train medical aid workers already
in the field. Because the usual screening methods were too
expensive and complex in countries with poor health-care facilities, they were using a simpler method.

The technique of wiping the cervix with diluted aceti
acid—vinegar, to give it its common name—was both simpl

and cheap. The acetic acid turned tissue containing precancerous and cancerous cells white so that they could be detected through visual inspection. Any woman suspected of having an abnormality could then be referred for further tests to one of the new primary care clinics which were being set up throughout the country.

It would be a couple of years before the system was running smoothly but Meg was as keen as the others to make sure that proper training was given to everyone involved in the project. Now she made sure that the young woman who was sitting in on their session that morning understood the procedure and what she was looking for.

'After swabbing the cervix with the diluted acid, you must check carefully for any signs which indicate there might be a problem.' She smiled reassuringly at the patient, a young woman named Sabatu, who was in her mid-thirties. 'This won't take long, Sabatu. Just relax.'

The young woman smiled as she settled back on the couch while Meg carefully carried out her examination, using a speculum to widen the opening to her vagina. She swabbed the area with the diluted acid then checked it carefully. She couldn't detect any abnormalities and was able to pass on the good news to the patient.

'That all looks fine, Sabatu. Thank you. But make sure that you visit your clinic in a couple of years' time and have another check-up. It really is important.'

Sabatu climbed gracefully down from the couch. 'Thank you, Dr Meg,' she said quietly. She spoke wonderful English and had told them that she'd been a teacher at one of the mission schools before it had been closed down, and that she was hoping to start teaching again once the school was re-opened. 'My mother died of cervical cancer and I do not want the same thing to happen to me, you understand.'

'I do, indeed. Having the tests done at regular intervals will help enormously. Cervical cancer can be treated effectively so long as it's detected at an early stage.'

Meg sighed as the young woman took her leave. 'That must

be one saying we all repeat over and over, worldwide. It's so frustrating when a woman dies of cervical cancer when it can be treated so successfully.'

Miriam Dupré, the aid worker, gave a very Gallic shrug. 'Women seem to think it is wrong to take time to care for themselves, *oui*? They are always too busy caring for everyone else!'

Meg laughed ruefully as she stripped the paper sheet off the couch. 'That just about sums it up! We're our own worst enemies, aren't we?' She checked her watch. 'Anyway, how about lunch? We can run through this again while we eat if you have any more questions, although you've seen how simple it is.'

'That will be good. Will Jack be there, too?' Miriam smiled pensively. 'Not that I am wanting to ask him too many questions about our work, you understand? It would be a shame to waste all our time on such matters.'

The lilt in her voice told Meg very clearly what Miriam would have liked to spend her time doing. She forced herself to smile but it was an effort all the same. The other woman's obvious interest in Jack made her feel extremely *possessive*! Not that she had any right to feel that way, of course. No right whatsoever, in fact. That thought didn't help one bit.

'We'll have to wait and see. I rather think there's some sort of crisis so he might be too busy to bother about lunch.'

There was a definite hint of *so there*! in her voice. She quickly turned away when she saw the other woman give her a speculative look. 'Anyway, come along, Miriam. We'll go and see what we can rustle up.'

'*Merci*, Meg. And I apologise. I did not understand about you and Jack, you see.' Once again there was that Gallic shrug which said far more than it should have done. Meg hesitated, wondering if she should set the Frenchwoman straight. After all, there was no *her* and Jack, not in those terms, anyway.

The urge to be fair lasted less than a second before Meg smiled and gave a shrug of her own, leaving it up to Miriam to interpret it however she chose. She hadn't actually told a *lie*, she told herself to quieten her noisy conscience when Miriam uttered a regretful sigh. She'd just put a slight *spin* on the facts, that was all.

Why? a small voice inside her head whispered. Why had she felt it necessary to do so? Could she have been jealous at the thought of the attractive Frenchwoman making a play for Jack?

She pushed open the kitchen door with a touch more force than was necessary, refusing to answer either of those questions. What was it the Americans said when they didn't want to answer a question in a court of law, that they would plead the Fifth Amendment? Well, she was doing so now!

Lunch was nearly over when Jack appeared, looking very grim. Miriam perked up as soon as she saw him but he didn't appear to have noticed she was there, Meg realised with a satisfaction she certainly shouldn't have felt. However, such shameful thoughts soon fled when she realised that they had a crisis on their hands.

'Bill Tranter is in the hospital bay. He's not at all well from the look of him,' Jack announced bluntly.

'What's wrong with him?' Meg asked, getting up to pour Jack a cup of tea. Bill was the train's chief engineer and driver, a pleasant man in his late forties who adored his job. He spent all his free time fiddling with various bits of machinery to ensure that it continued running smoothly. Consequently, Meg had only spoken to him half a dozen or so times but she was concerned to hear this unexpected news.

'I'm not sure yet. I've taken bloods and Alison is going to run them through all the usual tests. Bill's feverish and wheezing badly. He's very lethargic and has a lot of muscle pain.' Jack ran his hand round the back of his neck and sighed. 'He was on the verge of passing out when Lesley found him in the corridor.'

'Maybe malaria?' Meg suggested thoughtfully.

'I wondered about that but the symptoms aren't quite right…' Jack shook his head. 'Anyway, Bill swears he's been taking his antimalarial tablets and Sam backs him up,' he added, referring to the other man who helped keep the train running smoothly.

'Then let's hope Alison comes up with something, although I don't know what's going to happen if Bill is ill for any length of time,' Meg observed worriedly. 'Who's going to drive the train for us? The local men he's been training haven't got enough experience yet, I wouldn't have thought.'

'That's my main concern, too. We're going to be really stuck if Bill is out of action for very long. The whole success of this mission rests on him being fit enough to carry on driving for us.' Jack shook his head. 'Just when things were going so well, too.'

'Maybe you could ask for someone else to fly out here and help you?' Miriam suggested with a charming smile. 'There must be some other person who can drive this train, *n'est-ce pas*?'

'That's what I'm hoping if it comes down to it.' Jack's smile was warm when he looked at the Frenchwoman. Meg felt a spurt of irritation when she saw it. She quickly clamped down on the feeling as she excused herself and went to see how Bill was doing. It wasn't right to feel so possessive about Jack. Neither had it been right to mislead Miriam the way she had. What was happening to her? Why was she acting this way?

She pushed open the hospital bay door with a sigh. So many questions and so few answers. One day soon she would get it all sorted out with a bit of luck!

Lesley had just finished giving Bill a drink when Meg arrived. He managed a wobbly smile but it was obvious that he was feeling very ill.

'Sorry about this,' he muttered between wheezing coughs. 'I feel a right fool, letting you all down.'

'Don't be silly, Bill. You can't help being ill.' Meg nodded when Lesley muttered about getting something to eat. She pulled over a chair and sat down as the other woman hurried away. Katu was fast asleep and she had a few minutes to spare before going back to work.

'I don't suppose so but it still feels wrong to be lying here.' Bill coughed violently again then sank weakly back against the pillows. 'Not that I'd be much help in this state. What's worrying me is how you're going to manage with me laid up. Those chaps aren't ready to drive the train without supervision.'

'Maybe Sam could supervise them?' Meg suggested, not wanting him to worry.

'Oh, I don't know about that.' Bill didn't sound too keen on the idea so Meg didn't pursue it. It was obvious that he was feeling pretty rotten so she didn't stay long and just made sure that he had everything he needed before she left him to rest.

Jack and Miriam were already in the consulting room, examining another patient. Meg felt a bit like a spare part when the Frenchwoman claimed his attention by asking endless questions. Any scruples Miriam might have had about cutting in had obviously flown out of the window, Meg thought sourly, handing the other woman a dish of diluted acetic acid.

Her mouth thinned at the thought and she turned away, only to pause when she caught sight of the twinkle in Jack's eyes. What did he have to laugh about? she wondered, sending up a fervent prayer that she wasn't the source of his amusement. Did Jack suspect that she was annoyed because the other woman was paying him so much attention?

The idea was like a dousing of cold water. She kept her mind firmly on her work for the rest of the day!

'There's nothing shown up so far. Of course, it needs a bit longer to complete all the tests but I think we can safely rule out malaria.'

It was early the next morning and Alison had popped in with the results of Bill's blood tests she'd managed to collect so far. Jack sighed as he sank onto the end of the examination couch and read through her findings.

'So I see. There's no trace of microorganisms in the cultures either. I just wish I knew what was wrong with him,' he declared.

'Maybe it's some sort of non-specific viral infection,' Meg suggested as Alison hurried away.

'Maybe. But I don't want to be too hasty by making assumptions. Let's go and take another look at him, shall we? Then put our heads together and see if we can come up with the right answer.' Jack grinned as he opened the door for her. 'Two heads are better than one, or so the saying goes.'

Meg laughed softly. Jack had been in a surprisingly good mood that morning, given the problems they faced with Bill out of action. They had been due to move from their present location that day but now that wouldn't be possible. Sam had made no bones about the fact that he didn't think he was experienced enough to supervise the trainee drivers so that had put paid to that idea.

Maybe Jack had come up with another solution and that was the reason for his buoyant mood? she thought as she followed him to the hospital bay. Or maybe it was the fact that Miriam had stayed to have dinner with them the night before and had continued to pay Jack an inordinate amount of attention? a small voice whispered. Hadn't he said something about trying to get his personal life together? Perhaps he'd made a start on it already.

Her own happy mood swiftly evaporated. It was an effort to smile at Lesley and Katu who were playing noughts and crosses. It was fast becoming one of Katu's favourite games and all of them took turns to play it with her whenever they had a few minutes to spare.

She joined Jack by Bill's bed, careful to keep her face free of expression. It wasn't nice to realise that she could feel jealous because she'd never believed herself to be that sort of a person. However, she soon put her own problems to the back of her mind when she saw how ill poor Bill looked.

There was no doubt that he was worse that morning, she thought worriedly, noticing how grey and drawn he looked as he lay there, coughing. She checked his chart when Jack silently handed it to her and saw immediately that his temperature was extremely high. However, he tried to put on a cheerful face when he saw them.

'Two of you today, eh? Don't know if that's a good or a bad sign.'

Jack grinned. 'Only the best for one of our own, Bill. You know that.' He pulled over a chair, indicating that Meg should do the same. 'Right, let's go through everything you've done since you arrived in Oncamba. There has to be a reason why you're ill so let's find it, shall we?'

Bill groaned. 'Now you're asking! Don't know if I can remember half the things I've done, to be honest.'

'Give it a try, Bill. It might help.' Meg added her encouragement to Jack's and earned herself a smile. She sat on the chair, enveloped in a warm glow. It was pathetic really. All it took was a smile or a few words of praise and she was like an eager puppy, lapping them up! However, it didn't make a scrap of difference, even knowing that.

Bill related what he had done since he'd arrived in Oncamba. It took him some time in between bouts of coughing and sips of water. It was when he came to a bit about how he and Sam had gone swimming that Jack cut in.

'When was this?'

'Oh, four—five weeks ago. We'd been working flat out to make sure everything was ready for when you arrived. One of the aid workers we'd met up with told us about this lake where they all went swimming, so we decided to have an afternoon off and go along there.'

Bill took another sip of water. 'Anyway, in the end, Sam decided not to go into the water as he's not much of a swimmer but I went in and really enjoyed it.' He frowned. 'Can't have caught anything from that water, surely? It looked clean enough and other people had swum there.'

'I can't say for certain but it could be the key we're looking for. Do you know where these aid workers are stationed?' Jack stood up after Bill had told him the name of the town. 'It's definitely worth checking out. You have a rest now, Bill. I'll be getting in touch with your firm and suggesting they fly you home. I think that would be the best thing for you, although we'll be sorry to lose you.'

'Aye, expect you're right.' Bill sounded resigned as he closed his eyes. It was obvious that he felt too ill to object. Meg followed Jack out to the corridor.

'What do you think it is?' she asked, watching him closely. 'You have an idea, don't you?'

'I do. I could be wrong but I don't think so. Katayama fever. Ever heard of it?'

Meg frowned. 'Something to do with snails, I think.' She saw his surprise and laughed. 'I did some reading up on tropical diseases after I heard I'd be working for the agency.'

'Good for you.' His smile was warm and once again Meg found herself basking in it.

'You're right, anyway. Katayama fever is an acute form of schistosomiasis, a parasitic disease. It's contracted through contact with fresh water that harbours the snail hosts. The schistosomes produce eggs that hatch into larvae which pass into the snails. Eventually, the larvae leave the snails and burrow through the skin of anyone swimming in the water. They get into the bloodstream and eventually settle into the bladder and intestines where they mature into adult worms. They, in turn, lay eggs which trigger the sort of symptoms we've seen here.'

Jack sighed. 'It's a big problem throughout Africa and parts of India as well. Katayama fever is particularly difficult to diagnose as there are no definitive serological or immunological tests. However, I'll get Alison to check the presence of eosinophilia in those blood samples. A rise in the number of white cells which react with eosin dye is an indication of parasitic infection, amongst other things. It would confirm if I'm on the right track.'

'At least we'll know what we're dealing with, then,' Meg said thankfully. 'Although it sounds horrible!'

'It is. It can be very nasty indeed.' Jack frowned thought

fully. 'If Bill has been taken ill, it seems likely that some of
the aid workers might also be suffering from the same trouble.'

'They're going to need treatment, too, aren't they?' Meg
said in concern. 'That could be a problem if they don't realise
what's wrong with them.'

'It certainly could. I need to get over there and see them
straight away, warn them of the dangers and treat anyone
who's become infected. We'll start Bill on praziquantel at a
rate of 20 mg per kilo of body weight, twice a day for the
next three days. That should kill off the parasites, although
he'll probably need subsequent treatment.'

'He'll get that in hospital, won't he? When he returns to
England. Will you be able to get in touch with his firm and
make the arrangements?'

'Yes. I'll do it at the same time as visiting the aid workers.'
He sighed. 'I may as well leave straight away because it's
obvious we won't be going anywhere today. In fact, I think
I'm going to tell everyone that we're having a day off. It will
do everyone good to have a rest.'

'You're not going to get much rest if you're driving round
the country,' Meg observed.

'Don't worry about me. I'm used to it.'

It was on the tip of her tongue to tell him that she couldn't
help worrying but she knew that would be the wrong thing to
say. She didn't have the right to worry about him, just as she
didn't have the right to feel possessive.

Meg sighed as Jack hurried away to get everything organised. There were an awful lot of things she didn't have the
right to do where Jack was concerned and it bothered her.

The time seemed to drag after Jack had left. Lesley and Kate
decided to go to the village as there was a wedding being held
there that day. Miriam had invited them over and asked Meg
as well, but she'd made some sort of excuse not to go.

She was still a bit wary of the Frenchwoman after the previous day. Not that she had any real reason to be, of course.
Jack had every right in the world to enjoy the other woman's

company and she had no say in the matter. After all, she'd been the one to urge him to start living again, hadn't she?

That depressing thought seemed to set her on a downward spiral so that by the time she heard the Land Rover returning late that evening she was feeling very down in the dumps. However, it would have been unforgivable to let Jack see that she'd missed him so she didn't go hurrying to meet him when the others did.

Meg sat by herself in the lounge, moodily flicking through a magazine while she listened to the chatter flowing in from the corridor. The wedding celebrations were continuing that night and everyone was going back to the village to join in the fun, apart from her. She'd volunteered to stay behind and care for their patients and the others had been only too pleased to accept her offer. Now she glanced up as Jack poked his head round the door.

'Lesley says you're not going to the festivities,' he observed quietly. He looked tired, she noticed immediately, his eyes ringed with heavy circles, his skin grey-tinged with fatigue. Travelling throughout Oncamba by road was a gruelling experience and he must have covered almost fifty miles that day. However, she doubted if he would appreciate her sympathy so she didn't offer it.

'Someone has to stay behind,' she said lightly. 'I volunteered.'

'Well, now I'm back you can go with the others. I'm too tired to go anywhere else tonight so I'll be here to keep an eye on things.'

Was that a subtle way of telling her that he would prefer to have the place to himself? Meg wasn't sure, but there was no way she was going to be accused of having a thick skin!

She tossed the magazine onto the seat beside her and stood up. 'Fine by me.'

'Meg?' Jack stopped her when she went to storm past him. There was a faint puzzlement darkening his eyes, a hint of uncertainty in the look he gave her as he drew her to a halt with a firm hand on her arm.

'What did I say?' He shook his head when she opened her mouth. 'No, I can tell you're annoyed. I know you well enough by now to recognise the signs!'

Did he? And what else could he tell? Could he tell how confused she was about the way she acted around him? Could he explain why she felt this way? He was a darn sight cleverer than she was if he could!

'I'm not annoyed,' she declared in a clipped tone. She stared pointedly at his hand. 'If you don't mind…'

'Oh, but I do. I mind very much. I want to know what's wrong and I want you to tell me.' His hand slid up her arm. Maybe he'd just been making sure she couldn't walk away but it had felt more like a caress than anything else. Meg heard the gasp that left her lips as clearly as Jack obviously did it.

'Meg, I…' He stopped when Lesley suddenly appeared. Letting go of Meg, he turned to the other woman with a smile which seemed a trifle strained. 'Ready for off, then?'

'Yes. Just checking that Meg doesn't mind being left behind,' Lesley replied, glancing at her. Meg opened her mouth, but before she could answer Jack cut in.

'I just told her that I'll look after things here so she can go and enjoy herself.'

He turned towards the door with an exaggerated groan. 'Meanwhile, I can think of nothing more tempting than a hot shower to ease the knots out of my spine!'

Lesley laughed sympathetically as he headed for the bathroom. 'He must be black and blue after that drive! Anyway, come along. Time to join in the fun.'

She whisked Meg along the corridor and down the steps, giving her no time to think let alone protest. But protest against what? Joining the others for a night of fun and laughter? Enjoying herself without worrying about Jack and how he made her feel for once? She should have been eager to go along now that she had the chance to do so and yet she found her footsteps faltering.

'I…I'll catch you up. I just need to…to have a word with

Jack about…about Katu,' she improvised when Lesley looked at her.

'OK. Don't be long, though, or you'll miss all the fun!' Lesley waved as she hurried away. It was only a short distance to the village and Meg could hear the music from where she stood as the celebrations got under way. She knew that she would have no difficulty finding her way there later. However, right at that moment it seemed imperative that she sort out this situation and get things straight in her own head if nothing else. What did she feel about Jack? How did he feel about her? Maybe it was time she found out what the answers were.

She took a deep breath before she climbed back on board the train. Everywhere was almost eerily quiet now that the others had left. Apart from the muted sound of water running in the bathroom, there was very little noise. Meg went first to the hospital bay but both Bill and Katu were fast asleep.

She made her way back along the corridor, wondering how best to approach this. She couldn't just come out and ask Jack how he felt about her because she didn't have the nerve. Equally, she couldn't tell him how she felt because she wasn't sure! Suddenly, the idea of confronting him seemed less appealing than it had done a few minutes earlier because she was beset by doubts. She might simply be making a bad situation worse!

Meg swung round as panic hit her. She took a few hasty steps towards the nearest exit then ground to a halt when the bathroom door opened and Jack appeared. He was dressed only in a towel, wrapped tightly around his narrow hips, and his black hair was dripping water.

Meg's mouth went dry as she stood there, unable to move and watched the droplets running down his muscular chest. Suddenly every rational thought seemed to have evaporated. She had no idea at all how to answer when Jack said softly, 'So, Meg, what are you doing back here? Was there something you wanted?'

CHAPTER NINE

YOU!

For one horrified second Meg wondered if she'd said it out loud. However, a glance at Jack's face reassured her that she hadn't. She took a shallow breath and tried to stifle the noise her heart was making as it bounced around inside her ribcage.

'I…um…I just wanted to know how you'd got on,' she hurriedly improvised. She saw one of Jack's brows wing upwards and rushed on. 'Were any of the aid workers ill? And did you manage to contact Bill's employers? Oh, and how about Katu? Did you—?'

'Whoa!' Jack held up his hand. There was a rueful smile on his mouth but it didn't quite disguise the satisfaction she could see there as well.

Meg frowned as she wondered what on earth he had to look *satisfied* about before she realised he was still speaking.

'Give me a chance to put on some clothes then I'll fill you in on everything that's happened. Think you can wait five minutes for your answers?'

Meg blushed when she realised he was teasing her. 'Of course,' she replied stiffly. 'Would you like a cup of coffee? I could make it while you're getting dressed.'

'That would be great. I don't suppose there's a chance of something to eat as well?' His tone was unashamedly wheedling and she laughed.

'I suppose I could rustle something up!'

'Great! Thanks, Meg.' His smile was oddly tender as he looked at her for a moment before he made his way to his compartment. Meg took another small breath and forced her shaky legs to carry her to the kitchen. They were reluctant to do so, very reluctant indeed, but she made them obey her. She

135

could hardly stand there like a lovesick puppy, waiting for Jack to return!

One of the villagers had brought them some eggs that morning as a gift so she quickly set about making an omelette, adding some of the canned luncheon meat they'd had for their meal that night plus some leftover vegetables. It was ready to serve by the time Jack appeared a few minutes later.

His brows arched when she put the plate in front of him. 'Spanish omelette?'

Meg shook her head so that the ponytail into which she'd fastened her hair that night bounced from side to side. 'Nope. *Oncamban* omelette!'

Jack laughed as he picked up his knife and fork. 'Well, it looks…' he forked up a mouthful and chewed it appreciatively '…and tastes delicious, whatever nationality it is!'

Meg smiled as she took two mugs from the cupboard and filled them with coffee. 'Good. Omelettes are one of my specialities.'

'I can tell.' He didn't say anything else as he tucked into the food. It didn't take him long to finish the omelette, making Meg realise just how hungry he must have been.

'There's some tinned peaches as well if you want them,' she offered immediately.

'Please.' He sat back in his chair with a sigh. 'I've had nothing to eat all day and I'm famished.'

'You shouldn't go so long without eating,' she said worriedly, getting up to put some of the fruit into a bowl. The train was equipped with a small refrigerator and the peaches were nicely chilled when she placed the dish in front of him.

'It wasn't intentional.' Jack spooned up a succulent slice of peach and ate it with obvious relish. 'Mmm, delicious!'

Meg sat down again and picked up her mug of coffee. 'I take it that you found the aid workers, then?'

'I did.' Jack sighed as he toyed with the fruit. 'Three of them were taken ill last week and were exhibiting much the same symptoms as Bill. Two were in a very sorry state, suffering diarrhoea and rectal bleeding as well. I prescribed praziquantel plus prednisolone twice daily for the next three days. I also suggested that the worst sufferers be sent home, which caused a bit of an uproar. However, it's in their best interests so I hope they take my advice.'

Meg could tell he was concerned and hurried to reassure him. 'I'm sure they will. The agencies responsible for sending them to Oncamba won't take any chances with their health.'

'No, I don't imagine they will.' Jack smiled. 'Thanks, Meg. That helps ease my mind. I felt so guilty about leaving those poor people there at the camp but I had to get back here.'

'You can't be in two places at once, Jack. Now finish your meal.'

'Yes, Nurse!' There was a twinkle in his eye which took the sting out of the remark. He cut into a peach then offered her the spoon. 'Here, have a taste—they're delicious.'

'Oh, no, they're for you...' she began, then sighed when she saw him narrow his eyes at her. 'Well, just a bite, then.'

She leant forward and opened her mouth while Jack carefully slid the morsel of fruit between her lips. The peach was deliciously sweet and ripe, the juice trickling down her throat as she bit into it. A little juice must have spilled off the spoon because she felt it run from the corner of her lips and hunted in her pocket for a tissue to wipe it away.

'Let me.' There was a husky note in Jack's voice as he reached across the table and wiped away the smear of juice with the tip of his finger. Meg's heart began to thump when she saw him raise his hand to his own mouth and lick away the sweetness with his tongue. There was something deeply, shockingly erotic about the thought of Jack tasting the juice which had been on her lips just a moment before.

She looked down at her coffee, afraid that he would see how disturbed she felt. The pulsing of her heart seemed to be spreading through her whole body, moving deeper and deeper inside her so that she could feel its beat echoed in other parts of her. She shifted uncomfortably when she felt the throbbing settle low in the pit of her stomach then felt it move lower still...

'Should arrive on Thursday. It couldn't have worked out better, in fact, although I doubt Bill will agree with me.'

Meg raised dazed eyes to Jack's face while she struggled to get a grip on herself. However, the force of the sensations she was experiencing shocked her. She wasn't totally inexperienced, neither was she näive enough to believe that it was only men who felt this kind of physical desire. Nevertheless, the fact that she felt it now, with such little reason, shocked her.

All Jack had done was wipe away a trickle of juice from her lips, for heaven's sake! Yet it felt as though it had been the prelude to something far more intimate. It was an effort to concentrate on the conversation as she realised that he was waiting for her to say something.

'You…you managed to get in touch with his firm, did you?' Her voice was husky to the point of hoarseness and she saw his eyes glitter hotly before he quickly looked away.

'Yes. I was able to contact them from the camp. They're going to arrange for an air ambulance to fly Bill home. In fact, we'll be able to solve two problems for the price of one.'

Jack's voice grated as well, sending frissons of awareness down Meg's spine when she heard it. She struggled on, knowing how dangerous it would be to let her mind wander at this point. To try and work out why he sounded so edgy would be a huge mistake in her present state of mind!

'Two problems? What do you mean?'

He pushed the dish of peaches away from him with a hint of impatience, as though he blamed them for what was going on. 'Bill's company has agreed to fly Katu back with him in the air ambulance. I managed to contact Patrick Wilde as well while I was there, and he immediately agreed to treat her.'

Jack shrugged but it was blatantly obvious that he was struggling to maintain his composure as well. 'Our office is going to contact the authorities and get clearance for her to enter the country.'

'Will they be able to do that in such a short space of time? I…I thought it took months…' Her voice trailed off because it was simply too hard to keep on talking when her heart wasn't in it. Of course she cared what happened to Katu and wanted only the best for her, but it was impossible to continue the conversation when the air was so charged with emotion.

When Jack pushed back his chair and stood, she jumped, her heart rebounding wildly inside her when she saw the grim expression on his face. Was he angry with himself because he couldn't detach himself from his emotions as he wanted to do? Was he angry with her because she was the reason for his lack of control? She had no idea but, as she rose to her feet, Meg knew that she had to make him see how wrong either of those reasons were!

'Jack, I—' she began, only to stop as he cut her off.

'I'm tired. I'm sure you'll understand if I have an early night.' He turned to leave then paused. 'Don't worry about Bill and Katu. I'll set my alarm and check on them in a couple of hours.'

'I understand, Jack.' She gave a small laugh, wincing when she heard the shrill edge it held, the hurt, the pain. 'Don't worry about having to get up to check on them. I don't feel much like partying, to tell the truth, so I'll be here if they need anything.'

She gave him a tight little smile, her eyes skating over his face. She wasn't strong enough to let herself look at him because she knew what she would see.

Tears suddenly blurred her vision and she stumbled as her foot caught on the table leg when she hurried towards the door. Jack caught hold of her arm to steady her, but even then she wouldn't look at him. Consequently, she wasn't prepared when he hauled her towards him with a muttered curse.

'You make me so mad, Meg! You make me feel things I swore I would never feel again!' The words were bitten out, laced with anger and a whole lot of other things that brought her reluctant gaze straight to his face. She felt a quiver run through her, then another and another until she was trembling as she saw the desire which had darkened his eyes and set a rim of colour along his angular cheek-bones.

'Jack?' she whispered, dry-mouthed with shock.

'Meg?' he mimicked, smiling with a tenderness she would never have expected. Cupping her face between his big warm hands, he brushed away her tears with his thumbs then slowly and with exquisite gentleness kissed her.

Meg felt an explosion of heat and light erupt inside her. It flowed through her veins, setting light to every cell in her body. She gasped in shock then gasped again in delight when Jack's arms tightened while he drew her even closer and deepened the kiss. The hungry plundering of his tongue seemed to release her from the spell that had fallen over her.

She twined her arms around his neck and returned the kiss with equal fervour, her tongue darting and dancing into his mouth, teasing, tormenting, seducing his. It was just a kiss and yet there seemed to be so much encompassed in it that she was afraid when he tried to end it.

She held him tightly, not wanting to let him go, not wanting to be back at square one, wondering and waiting, confused by her own feelings as well as his. He suddenly stopped pulling away and pulled her closer instead, kissing her again and again, letting his mouth say everything he either couldn't or wouldn't say. *It* was telling her that he wanted her, desired her, and that was all she needed to hear. Rational words would come later!

When Jack's hands slid down her body in that first seeking caress, she felt her heart stop from sheer pleasure. Yet when his fingers moved slowly upwards and found her aching breasts, it started racing again. Meg could feel its heavy beat pulsing through her and knew that Jack had felt it, too, but they were both too caught up in the magic they were creating together to worry about it.

His breath exhaled on a sigh when he felt her nipples pressing so eagerly into his palms but then Meg heard herself sigh as well. She closed her eyes, letting her mind spin and twist like a kaleidoscope in ever-changing patterns. There were simply too many sensations to absorb, to enjoy, to marvel at, to think clearly.

'You know where this is leading, Meg, don't you?' Jack's voice was barely above a whisper because it would have demanded too much effort for him to speak any louder.

Meg knew how he felt because speaking seemed such a waste when there were other things to concentrate on. She simply smiled at him, her eyes heavy with passion and invitation.

'Meg!' Her name on his lips sounded so wonderful, so right. When he swept her up into his arms she felt no qualms. She knew what was happening and it was what she wanted.

Jack carried her down the corridor and kicked open the door to his compartment then set her gently on her feet. There was no light in the small room apart from the glow from the moon as it filtered through the tiny porthole window, but it was bright enough to see by.

Reaching out, Meg unbuttoned his shirt and her hands didn't tremble at all. She had no doubts about what she was doing, which should have been surprising after all the heart-searching she'd done lately. She wanted Jack to make love to her. She wanted it more than anything she had ever wanted in her whole life.

She slid the shirt partly off his shoulders then got distracted by the sight of his muscular chest. Leaning forward, she rained a shower of tiny, sipping kisses across his warm, sleek skin.

'Meg!'

His voice was raw with emotion but not with anything to indicate that he wanted her to stop so she carried on, letting her lips travel where they chose, kissing, sipping, drinking in his taste and his warmth until suddenly she was trembling as hard as he was.

Jack caught hold of her shoulders and set her away from him. His eyes looked like jet in the moonlight. 'My turn.'

He took hold of the hem of her white cotton T-shirt and slowly drew it upwards, taking his time as he bared her body to his gaze. Meg shivered when she felt his eyes sweep over her. All she had on now was a lacy bra which did little to conceal the fullness of her breasts and that was soon dispensed with.

'You are so beautiful, Meg. But, then, I knew that you would be…'

His head dipped and a moan of pleasure escaped from her when his mouth found her breast. The gentle rasp of his tongue made her tremble so hard that she would have fallen if he hadn't supported her. Her head fell back and her eyes closed as a wave of passion swept through her, so intense, so fierce that she could barely believe what she was feeling. But maybe this was how love always felt, hot and wild, hungry and urgent, yet tempered by a tenderness which was probably the most potent feeling of all.

She loved Jack. Standing there in his arms at that moment, she finally acknowledged it. Suddenly she needed so much to tell him how she felt that any doubts about the wisdom of doing so disappeared.

'Jack, I—'

'Hello! Jack? Are you there?'

The sound of Miriam's voice was a cruel intrusion. Meg felt her heart stumble to a halt when she heard it. She wanted to tell Jack to ignore it, to pretend they weren't there and not answer, but it was too late for that, she realised when she felt him stiffen.

He drew back abruptly and looked at her. For a moment his eyes were full of everything she had felt, before he made an obvious effort to collect himself. And it was the fact that he could do so after the intensity of the passion they'd shared which hurt the most.

'I'd better see what she wants,' he said tersely.

'Yes, of course.' Meg turned away, afraid that he would see her despair. Picking up her T-shirt, she dragged it over her head before she turned round again.

'Are you all right?' he asked flatly.

'Of course. Why shouldn't I be?' Her tone was diamond-bright, the smile she gave him matching it perfectly.

He shrugged. 'No reason.' His tone was equally assured. He

started to open the compartment door then paused. 'About what happened just now, Meg…'

'Oh, don't worry about it!' She gave a tinkly laugh. 'I don't intend to!'

'Fine.' One last quick smile and then he was gone. Meg took a deep breath before she went to her own compartment and closed the door. She went to the window and stared into the night while her heart seemed to crack wide open.

How ironic to discover that she had fallen in love with Jack at that point. It would have been so much easier if it had struck her out of the blue one day while they were in the clinic, perhaps, rather than have it happen in the throes of passion. Maybe then she would have been able to rationalise it away, convince herself that she was mistaken, but she couldn't do that now.

No, she knew how she'd felt when he'd kissed her and *almost* made love to her. She wasn't going to be able to convince herself that she'd made a mistake. She also knew that Jack didn't feel the same way about her. He couldn't possibly do so if he'd been able to switch off his feelings so easily!

Oh, he might have *wanted* her, but that was all. He didn't love her. He never would. He'd given his heart once to a woman and had had it broken so he wasn't going to risk it happening again. It was better to accept that now than waste time wishing for the impossible…better, not easier, though!

'Right, I'll be back a.s.a.p., folks.' Rory gave them a cheery wave before he jumped down from the train. He had volunteered to drive to the newly cleared airstrip and meet the air ambulance when it landed. He would bring back the nurse who would accompany Bill and Katu back to England as well as the replacement driver. The airfield was a good hour's drive from where they were located but it could have been worse if Richard hadn't intervened. He'd been responsible for clearing the runway so that the plane could land, and everyone was grateful to him for that.

He'd arrived the previous evening with some of his men to

tell them the good news and had ended up staying overnight. Now Meg smiled at him as Rory roared away.

'Thank heavens Rory doesn't have to go all the way back to where we landed. It would have been a mammoth operation if you hadn't managed to get things organised.'

Richard treated her to his wonderful smile. 'I couldn't put you poor people through all that a second time. You might not agree to come here again if we don't treat you well!'

'Method in your madness, eh?'

Jack remarked with a laugh. However, Meg wasn't deaf to the note of restraint in his voice. It had happened a lot lately. Ever since that night, two days earlier, when they'd almost made love, Jack had been noticeably reserved whenever she was around. Now she excused herself, not wanting to dwell on why he should be behaving this way. If he regretted what had happened and felt guilty about it then she didn't want to know!

She went to the hospital bay where Bill was playing noughts and crosses with Katu. The pair had struck up a friendship and it was obvious that the man was very fond of the little girl. Katu clapped her hands in glee as she won yet another game and Meg hid a smile when Bill winked at her. Bill, like everyone else, usually let Katu win.

'So, how are you two doing?' she asked, perching on the end of the child's bed.

'Fine. I feel a right fraud, flying back home when there's nothing wrong with me,' Bill answered glumly.

'Don't be silly. I know you feel a lot better but you've been very ill. Jack has arranged for you to go straight to hospital where you'll have a thorough check-up and possibly more treatment. If it was Katayama fever then we have to be sure that it's been cleared up.'

'I expect you're right, love. It's just that I'll miss you lot, especially this little one—even though she does beat me all the time!'

Bill gave the little girl a hug. Katu responded with a happy smile. She had positively blossomed under all the attention, not to mention the intensive nursing care.

She looked so much better, Meg decided as she looked at the child's smiling face. If it weren't for the ugly wound on her leg it would have been fair to say that Katu was probably healthier than she'd been for a long time. It was obvious that she'd had barely enough to eat for some while. However, she was starting to put on weight now and her skin no longer had that lacklustre look. Once she'd had surgery to repair the wound she would be well on the road to a full recovery. Nonetheless, Meg was still very concerned about what would happen to her in the future.

The thought was very much on her mind all morning. Jack had decided that they would spend some time at the village, checking up on anyone who hadn't felt confident enough to visit them on board the train. Quite a number of people turned up for the impromptu clinic, although there were few really serious problems to deal with. However, Meg knew that treating small problems before they got the chance to grow bigger was always worthwhile.

She finished cleaning an ulcer on an old man's leg then dusted it with antibiotic powder and covered it with a dressing. Many of the villagers had ulcers. A combination of poor diet and the rapid spread of infection meant that cuts and scrapes often led to them. Richard had accompanied them to the village and he shook his head as the old man left.

'Conditions are even worse than I thought. It makes me feel guilty that I stayed away so long when I might have been able to do something sooner to help my people.'

Meg washed her hands with Hibiscrub and dried them on a paper towel. Jack had gone to visit an old woman who was unable to walk the short distance to where they were seeing patients, and Lesley had gone with him. The fact that he hadn't asked her to accompany him was a bit like having a wobbly tooth—she kept poking and prodding at the idea that he didn't want her anywhere near him despite how painful it was! It was a relief to concentrate on something other than her own problems when she heard what Richard had said.

'How long was the former ruler in power?'

'Almost fifteen years.' Richard grimaced as he went to the door and stared out. 'He was my uncle, my father's brother, but he wasn't a good man. I didn't want to come back here at first because I had a life in England and I was happy there.'

'What made you change your mind?' Meg asked quietly, taking a fresh pair of gloves from the box and slipping them on. There were another three people waiting patiently to be seen but she sensed that Richard wanted to talk so she didn't rush him.

'Oh, many things.' His expression was distant all of a sudden. 'I realised that there wasn't anything to keep me in England at the end of the day. I also realised that I couldn't stand back and watch my people suffering any longer if I could do something to help them. I came back to Oncamba and my uncle was deposed, although there are still a few of his supporters about who seem intent on making trouble.'

He shrugged. 'I have to be constantly on my guard because they would be only too happy to see me dead.'

'Good heavens! I hadn't realised that.' Meg couldn't hide her dismay and Richard grinned.

'Don't worry. I have no intention of letting them achieve their objective!'

He left the hut soon afterwards but Meg couldn't help wondering how he could be so calm about the situation. Funnily enough, she hadn't given any thought to the fact that there might be an unfriendly faction working within Oncamba. Everyone she'd met so far had been welcoming and grateful for their help, but there were always some, she surmised, who didn't like change even when it was for the better. Still, Richard didn't appear overly concerned so there didn't seem any point in her worrying about it.

They returned to the train at lunchtime. Meg was very conscious that Jack avoided speaking to her as they all walked back together. He kept up an easy conversation with Kate and

Lesley about some of the patients they'd seen that morning but ignored her.

Meg was hurt by his attitude but she refused to let him see that so she kept up a lively conversation with Richard, laughing as he told her about some of the problems he'd encountered since his return to Oncamba. Meg enjoyed their conversation and thought nothing of it until Jack stopped her as she was about to board the *Angel*.

'A word, please,' he said tersely.

'I'll put the kettle on.' Lesley moved on past them, chattering happily to Kate as they headed towards the kitchen. Alison and Guy were talking to Richard now and they disappeared along the corridor together.

Meg was very aware that she and Jack were on their own and her heart began to race as she wondered what he wanted to speak to her about. She soon found out.

'May I suggest that you concentrate on work instead of your social life,' Jack said curtly. 'I know it must be boring for a woman like you to have to think about your job virtually twenty-four hours a day, but you knew the odds before you came here.'

Social life? A woman like her?

Meg's lips moved but for a moment nothing came out. Questions were fighting for precedence, falling over each other like shoppers after bargains at a sale. It took a full sixty seconds before she managed to sort them into order and by then Jack had turned away.

'Hold it right there!' she ordered, her blue eyes glittering angrily when he looked round. 'You can't say something like that without explaining what you meant.'

'I should have thought it was obvious!' he snapped back. 'Oh, don't give me that *self-righteous* indignation, Meg! You and I both know that you were making a play for Richard just now.'

He laughed softly but the sound was devoid of amusement. Meg heard what it did hold, though, and her stomach lurched sickeningly as she recognised the contempt in his voice. 'I've been on the receiving end of it, don't forget. So I think I can claim to recognise the signs!'

'How dare you? How dare you accuse me of that?' Meg took a step towards him, uncaring what the others would think if they happened to see what was going on. All she could think about was the fact that Jack had dared to throw that back in her face as an insult.

Hadn't it meant anything to him the other night? Hadn't he realised that she'd been so eager to make love with him because it had meant something to her? Obviously not!

'Don't judge me by your former wife's actions, Jack Trent. I'm not Briony!'

She knew she'd gone too far the minute she saw his expression but she knew that she'd been justified in saying that. Jack *was* judging her by the other woman's actions…

Her heart seemed to stop when it hit her like a blinding flash that maybe he'd used the comparison before. To whom had Jack wanted to make love the other night? Her or Briony? Hadn't Alison remarked how like his ex-wife Meg was? She'd put that thought to the back of her mind but suddenly she realised how foolish she'd been to ignore it. If Alison had thought there was a physical resemblance between her and Briony, maybe Jack had noticed it, too?

It explained so much that had confused her in the past few weeks, from his animosity when they'd first met to the way he'd seemed to *respond* to her that night. But maybe it had all been a sham, a mockery. Jack hadn't been reacting to her, Meg Andrews, but to the memory of his ex-wife!

'I don't know what the hell you're talking about!'

Jack's expression was thunderous as he stared at her. Meg didn't care. She was too hurt to worry about angering him.

'No? Then think about it. Work it out, Jack. After all, you're a highly intelligent human being so it shouldn't be *that* difficult!'

'I have never, ever compared you to Briony!' he snapped Catching hold of her arm, he steered her round the front o the train, away from the open doorway.

Meg twisted her arm free and smiled coldly at him. 'No? Well, then, that's OK, isn't it? Obviously I'm mistaken. Still, I'm usually in the wrong so why worry, eh?'

He uttered what sounded like a curse under his breath. 'You would try the patience of a saint at times! I have never compared you to Briony and that's the truth whether or not you choose to believe it.' He gave a harsh laugh. 'I wouldn't insult you by making such a comparison. You're worth ten of my ex-wife, Meg!'

'I am?' She swallowed hard, feeling the anger drain from her. Jack gave a weary sigh as he looked down at the dusty ground.

'Yes. I made a mistake by marrying Briony and I don't deny it. I fell in love with an image, you see, not with a real woman. By the time I found out how foolish I'd been it was too late. We were already married by then and I knew that I had to try to make it work.'

He looked up and his eyes were empty all of a sudden. 'I'd taken my marriage vows in good faith, Meg. I wanted to keep them.'

'Only it wasn't possible to do that?' she asked quietly, her heart aching at the thought of what he must have been through.

Jack shrugged. 'No, not at the end of the day. There's a point in any relationship when you have to take a long, hard look at what's really happening. The reality was that Briony and I were two people with completely different goals in life. We had nothing in common once the passion died, which it did very quickly. Everything she held dear I considered unimportant, everything I felt was of value meant nothing to her. We were chalk and cheese in effect.'

'And you had no idea before you married?' Meg couldn't help asking, even though she sensed that it was something Jack had never spoken about before. She didn't want to hurt him but she needed to understand how his marriage could have gone so drastically wrong. Jack was so perceptive that she couldn't understand how he could have made such a huge mistake...

Unless it had been the passion he'd felt for his ex-wife which had knocked him off balance. The thought of him desiring the other woman to such an extent hurt so much, but she couldn't let him see how she felt.

'None whatsoever. I thought that Briony felt the same as I did about so many things that are important to me.' His tone was emotionless as he explained—he might have been discussing someone else rather than himself. Maybe that was the only way he could deal with the memories, Meg wondered, and that thought hurt as well. To know that his marriage still had the power to hurt him wasn't easy to deal with.

'Briony and I met when she agreed to do a modelling assignment for the aid agency. We organised a fashion show to raise funds and a lot of celebrities gave their support. Briony seemed fascinated by the work we did—she asked a lot of questions, offered her help if we needed it in the future.

'She phoned me after the show and we went out to dinner. One thing led to another and before long we were planning on getting married. She seemed so caring and concerned, so committed to everything I believed important.'

'But it was all an act?' Meg suggested softly.

'No, I don't honestly think it was deliberate. Briony is the sort of person who gets carried away by new ideas. She'd got it into her head that she wanted to become involved in helping the underprivileged and was simply swept along by her own enthusiasm. However, the reality came as a huge shock to her.

Jack laughed softly, with a hint of bitterness. 'I should have realised it would, but I wasn't thinking too clearly at the time, you understand.'

She did. She understood only too well and her heart ached even more. How she hated the thought of him loving the other woman to such an extent that his judgement had been impaired. However, there was nothing she could do to change what had happened in the past.

'When you mentioned the reality being different to what she expected, did you mean that Briony went on an aid trip with you?' she asked instead.

'Yes. I was due to go overseas a month after we were married and Briony begged me to let her go along. I was beginning to realise that I'd made a mistake by then but I thought…hoped…that it might help bring us together.'

He looked up at the sky and sighed. 'I thought there was a chance that she might come to understand why my work was so important to me but it was a disaster from the start. Briony couldn't cope with the heat, the dirt, the disease, the sheer ugliness of poverty. She stayed less than a week then returned to London. It was just a question of how long our marriage would last after that.'

'It must have been…painful for you,' Meg observed softly, wishing there was something she could say to take away the sadness from his expression.

'It was. It was also a salutary lesson.' He took a deep breath and his tone grated. 'I wouldn't ask any woman to share my life again. It wouldn't be fair on her.'

She knew what he was saying, that he was warning her they had no future, yet she couldn't let it go without trying to make him see that he was wrong. 'Not all women would react like Briony did, Jack.' She took a quick breath. 'I wouldn't.'

He smiled and there was tenderness in his eyes when he looked at her. 'I know that. However, it isn't a risk I intend to take ever again. The kind of life I lead isn't conducive to a healthy relationship. The constant separations would put a strain on it for starters, and no woman would choose to be constantly travelling the world from one disaster area to another. I won't put myself or any woman in that kind of situation again.'

What could she say when he'd made up his mind? Nothing. There was nothing she could say or do and the futility of the situation was more than she could bear.

Meg turned and walked away, uncaring where she was going or the fact that Jack called her name. She couldn't run from the pain she felt because it was locked deep inside her; she just couldn't bear to add to it. Jack had said that he hadn't compared her to Briony but he was still judging her by the other woman's actions!

A bitter laugh rose to her throat, grew bigger and bigger until it felt as though it would choke her. What a good job she hadn't told Jack that she loved him! At least her pride wasn't now in tatters along with her emotions. It was the only consolation she had.

CHAPTER TEN

RORY arrived back just as everyone was finishing lunch. Meg heard the Land Rover arriving and went out to meet him. She hadn't bothered with lunch because she hadn't been able to face the thought of seeing Jack. She needed to know that her emotions were firmly in check before she saw him again. However, as she left her compartment, she couldn't help wondering if it would be possible to control this pain she felt.

'Howdy, folks!' Rory climbed out of the Land Rover, grinning from ear to ear. 'I have a surprise for you.'

He opened the passenger door with a flourish. Meg frowned when she saw a slim, dark-haired young woman get out. It was obvious that Rory had been referring to his passenger, although she had no idea who she was.

'Yvonne!' Lesley supplied the answer as she let out a joyful shriek of welcome. Both she and Kate ran to meet the newcomer and were obviously delighted to see her.

'What are you doing here?' Kate demanded. 'You were supposed to be sick!'

'I was.' The young woman shrugged. 'But I'm feeling a lot better now, so when this job came up I volunteered for it.'

She smiled at the two women then suddenly caught sight of Meg. She came forward and held out her hand. 'Hi, I'm Yvonne Fleming. You must be the poor soul who got commandeered at the eleventh hour to replace me. I bet you've been cursing me roundly!'

'Not at all!' Meg denied with a laugh as she shook Yvonne's hand. 'I'm glad it wasn't anything too serious that stopped you coming on this trip, though.'

'Thankfully not.' Yvonne's smile wavered as her gaze was suddenly drawn to someone behind Meg.

Meg glanced round to see who Yvonne was looking at and realised that Richard had come to see what was happening. There was a short, uncomfortable silence before he spoke.

'Hello, Yvonne. It's good to see you again.'

'And you too, Richard.' Yvonne's expression said everything she obviously had no intention of saying out loud. Meg felt her own heart ache when she saw the sadness on the other woman's face. That there was a lot of painful history between Yvonne and Richard was blatantly obvious and yet, oddly, none of the others appeared to notice anything amiss. Maybe it was just she who had homed in on the undercurrents because her own situation made her receptive to them.

Her gaze drifted to Jack, who had gone to introduce himself to the other occupant of the Land Rover, a man in his late forties who had to be the replacement driver. She felt a sharp pain assail her and turned away before anyone noticed there was something wrong with her. However, it struck her how difficult it was going to be to act normally around Jack in the coming weeks. Knowing that she loved him and that he would never love her was going to put an intolerable strain on their working relationship.

'Right, come inside and have a cuppa before you do anything else.' Lesley linked her arm through Yvonne's and steered her towards the steps. Kate and Rory went with them, Rory complaining bitterly that he was famished as he hadn't eaten for *hours*. Jack had taken the new driver to meet Sam and Richard had disappeared somewhere or other.

Meg took a deep breath then determinedly made her way back on board. The only way she was going to get through the coming weeks was by concentrating on work so she may as well make a start right away.

She went to the hospital bay to prepare Bill and Katu for the drive back to the plane. The return flight was scheduled for the same day as there was no point in delaying. However, when she reached the hospital, she discovered that Bill was taking a shower and that Richard was sitting with Katu. The little girl was chattering away to him, obviously delighted have someone to talk to. She'd learned a few English words in the short time she'd been on board, mainly their names or the names of various things she wanted, but it must have been very hard on her, not being able to communicate in her own language.

Now Meg smiled when she saw how animated the child looked as she went to join them. 'It's lovely to see her smiling like that. It must be great for her to have someone to talk to.'

Richard made a determined effort to smile back but Meg could see the shadows in his eyes. 'She's a very brave little girl. Having to cope with what she's been through would be hard enough for an adult.'

He broke off as Katu said something to him. The child was holding a picture she'd drawn and obviously wanted him to relay what she was saying to Meg.

Richard nodded in agreement then turned to Meg. 'Katu wants you to have this picture. She said to tell you that you are the lady in it.'

Meg took it with a smile. 'Thank you, sweetheart.' She glanced at the brightly coloured drawing and laughed gently. 'Is it my imagination or do I have wings sprouting out of my back?'

'You have.' Richard pointed to a small figure in the drawing. 'That is supposed to be Katu herself when she was lying, injured. She said that she was so scared and then suddenly you came along, like an angel, and saved her.'

Richard's laugh was tender when he looked at the child. 'She was touched by an angel, she claims, and that angel was you, Meg.'

'I don't know what to say...' Meg's eyes filled. She quickly bent and gave the little girl a warm hug. 'Thank you, poppet. That is the nicest thing anyone has ever said to me.'

Richard relayed what she'd said to the child, who smiled happily. He stood up as Katu picked up her pad and began drawing another picture. 'Jack told me about her grandmother dying and that she has no other family who will look after her.'

'That's right.' Meg sighed as she glanced at the picture once more. 'I'm hoping that we can make some sort of arrangements for her long-term care after she's been treated, but I'm not sure what we'll be able to do.'

'I can help out there.' Richard shot a look at the little girl and his face was so sad that Meg's heart ached for him. 'I shall make sure that she is taken care of. There is plenty of room in my house so I shall arrange to have her flown back to Oncamba and live with me. I might never be lucky enough to have a family of my own so it will be good to know that I can help a child who needs it so much.'

He gave Meg a last sad smile before he left. Meg sighed as the door closed. Did Richard believe that he would never have a family of his own because the woman he loved, Yvonne, wouldn't be willing to make that kind of commitment?

She suspected that was the explanation and it was so sad. Being in love certainly wasn't easy, as she knew to her cost.

Richard left a short time later, claiming that there were matters that needed his urgent attention. Although Meg didn't doubt that was true, she guessed that his abrupt departure owed itself more to the fact that he found the situation between himself and Yvonne too painful to deal with.

Yvonne was conspicuous by her absence when everyone gathered to wave him off. Nobody commented on it, although Meg suspected that they all knew what was going on. When Jack announced that he would drive the party to the airfield and would like to leave straight away, there was a chorus of agreements. Meg guessed that everyone was keen to get on with the job they were there for, although for very different reasons.

Bill was hugged and kissed before he left, but it was Katu to whom everyone paid extra-special attention. Meg hadn't brought much in the way of jewellery with her but she had a small silver locket which her mother had bought her one Christmas. She knew her mother wouldn't mind in the least if she gave it to the little girl and was so pleased that she had when she saw Katu's face light up.

'You be a very good girl, now, won't you?' Meg hugged the frail little body to her, feeling tears burning her eyes. She laughed as she realised that the child had no idea what she was saying, but it didn't seem to matter. 'God bless, sweetheart.'

She kissed Katu on the cheek and received a hug in return which made her eyes fill all the more. She stepped back, trying to smile as Kate and Lesley came forward to kiss the child.

'She'll be fine, Meg. Promise.'

Jack's tone was so tender that her tears overflowed. She heard him sigh softly before he drew her aside. The Land Rover was parked close to the front of the train and he steered her across the track, out of sight of the others.

'Richard has promised to look after her, if that's what you're worried about,' he assured her gently.

'I know. He told me.' Meg sniffed back her tears, feeling like a fool. The problem was that it wasn't just Katu's departure which was so upsetting, but also everything else that had happened of late. It was as though a huge lake of emotion had filled up inside her and was starting to overflow.

'Then you should know that there isn't anything to get upset about.' Jack's tone was curt all of a sudden. He turned to go back and join the others but Meg stopped him, a puzzled frown darkening her brow.

'What's wrong now?' she asked. She shook her head when he opened his mouth to deny the accusation. 'No, I can tell something is wrong, Jack. I know you too well by now not to know when you're annoyed.'

'I'm not annoyed, Meg.' His tone was icily contained. Any trace of tenderness had dissipated like melting snow in the sun. 'I just hope you realise that Richard has a lot on his plate at present.'

'A lot on his plate…' She stared at him in confusion before it hit her what he meant. Suddenly she was so angry that she wanted to spit. She felt both furious and hurt by his refusal to see what was staring him in the face.

'Thank you for the warning, Jack. I'm sure you only wanted

to save me from getting hurt. However, I'm not the least bit interested in Richard in *that* way, as I've told you before.'

'No?' He gave a bitter laugh. 'I know what you *said* but it doesn't look like it from where I'm standing!'

'Then maybe you should get yourself a pair of glasses.' Meg tossed back her hair and glared at him. She was too incensed by the unjust accusation to care what she was saying. 'It couldn't be that you're jealous, Jack? Of course not! After all, you aren't interested in forming any close relationships, as you told me yourself, so why should you care what I do?'

'I care if it could create a problem within the team,' he snapped back, his eyes glittering warningly. However, Meg refused to heed the warning, even though she knew there was a strong chance that she would regret not doing so later.

'Ah, yes, the team. And that's all I am, of course. A member of this team. I'm nothing special to you. I'm not even a substitute for Briony, or so you claim, although I have my doubts. Was it really *me* you wanted to make love to the other night? Or was I really a substitute for her? You certainly seem determined to judge me by your ex-wife's standards all the time, despite your assertions to the contrary!'

He looked as though he'd been poleaxed for a moment. But he recovered fast. He took a quick step towards her and caught hold of her by the shoulders. Meg felt a frisson run down her spine when she saw the anger in his eyes. 'Damn you, Meg. How could you—?'

He got no further. Whatever he'd been about to say was cut off when a sudden burst of noise rang out across the countryside. Meg's heart missed a beat as she realised that what she'd heard had been the sound of gunshots.

'What the devil was that?' Jack demanded, as he let her go and ran back to the others.

Meg hurriedly followed him. 'Where did it come from?' she asked, stopping beside Lesley.

'I'm not sure... Over there by those trees, I think.' Lesley pointed towards a small stand of trees some distance away

Even as Meg turned to look there was another round of shots fired.

'Right, everyone back on board, *pronto*!' Jack rapped out. 'I want all the doors closed and locked from the inside. Then I want the shutters put up over every window. I've no idea who's firing those shots, but let's not take any chances.'

He turned to Bill. 'Can you make sure the new chap knows what's what? I want us ready to leave here as soon as possible if need be.'

'Will do.' A rather shaky Bill let Rory help him into the driver's cab.

Meg helped Kate get Katu back on board then hurried along the train, securing the doors. They hadn't closed the steel shutters over the windows since they'd boarded the train and some of them proved rather recalcitrant. However, they were all finally closed and the train was secure. She could hear the engine starting up, rumbling as it built up a head of steam. Whether they would be able to outrun any pursuers was open to question but she agreed with Jack's decision. Until they knew what was happening they couldn't afford to take any chances.

'Two trucks coming in fast from the direction of the woods!' Guy had been watching through a crack in one of the shutters. Everyone ran to take a look at what he had seen. Meg's mouth went dry when she saw the trucks heading towards them at some speed. Who was in them? Friend or foe?

'My heaven, it's Richard!' Jack's shout startled them all. Meg peered through the gap in the shutter and realised that he was right. The trucks were the ones Richard's men had been driving, although she could see no sign of him as they screeched to a halt. It was only when a couple of the men dropped the tailgate of one of the trucks that she spotted him, and her heart turned over when she realised that Richard had been injured.

'Get him in here fast!' Jack was first to reach the door. He unlocked it, his face settling into grim lines as Richard was carried on board. Blood was pouring from a wound high on

Richard's right thigh and from another in his right shoulder. He was unconscious and his skin was tinged grey from the amount of blood he'd lost.

'Richard! Darling!' Yvonne rushed to his side, her face filled with anguish as she took hold of his hand. Jack firmly moved her aside as he began rapping out orders.

'Kate, get scrubbed up and set up one of the theatres. Rory, you know what to do.' He turned to Meg. 'I want you to assist me. Lesley will assist Guy. Both teams will work simultaneously. OK?'

Meg didn't waste time asking questions as she hurried to get ready. By the time Richard was wheeled into Theatre a short time later, everything was set up.

'Guy, if you could take the wound to his shoulder, I'll deal with his leg.'

Jack didn't pause as he walked to the operating table. Richard's clothes had been cut away and it was easy to see where the bullet had entered his upper thigh. Meg cleaned the surrounding skin and covered it with a sterile drape then stood aside. It was hard to come to terms with the fact that just a half hour previously she'd been talking to Richard and now he was lying unconscious on the table. However, if Jack felt the same, he didn't allow it to affect his work.

As soon as he got the go-ahead from Rory, he began. 'Looks like a high-velocity rifle shot to me. See how deeply the bullet is embedded in the tissue.'

He carefully eased away a bit of cloth from Richard's trousers which had been carried into the wound when the bullet had entered his thigh. Meg could see then how deeply the bullet had embedded itself into the flesh.

'It's going to be difficult to get it out, isn't it?' she asked softly, studying the damaged tissue.

'It isn't going to be easy, let's just say,' Jack observed grimly. 'It's within a hairsbreadth of the femoral artery. Thank heavens it didn't hit it.'

Meg didn't say anything. There was no need. They both knew that if the bullet had cut through the artery Richard would have bled to death before his men could have got him to the train.

Jack worked steadily, cleaning and carefully abrading the damaged tissue until he reached the bullet. 'Forceps.'

Meg passed them to him then held her breath as he carefully withdrew the bullet and dropped it into a kidney dish. Guy was working away on Richard's shoulder while Rory constantly monitored the patient's condition. When Jack was sure that the wound was as clean as he could get it, he packed it with sterile gauze and covered it with a light dressing.

'I don't want to close it until I'm sure there's no sign of infection,' he explained to Meg. He stepped away from the table, a frown darkening his brow. 'I just hope to heaven that there's no other damage, but it's impossible to tell at this stage.'

Meg paused in her counting of the swabs they'd used. 'But there are only two bullet wounds.'

'Yes, but high-velocity gunshot injuries can cause damage to other organs as well because of the shock waves that pass through the body. We'll just have to keep a close eye on him to make sure nothing is amiss.'

He looked up as Guy came to join him. 'Everything OK your end?'

'I think so. First gunshot wound I've had to deal with, to be honest.' Guy looked momentarily worried.

Jack slapped him on the shoulder. 'Knowing you, it will be fine, Guy!'

The younger man smiled. He looked a lot more confident when he left the theatre. Meg smiled to herself, thinking how typical it was of Jack to worry about Guy's feelings. He was a good boss and a wonderful team leader who always got the best out of everyone. But, then, she might very well be biased!

Funnily, her heart felt lighter than it had done for a couple of days even though the situation was so dire. Just working alongside Jack, that seemed to lift her spirits and give her hope. Maybe she'd misread the situation and he hadn't viewed her as a substitute for his ex wife the other night after all.

Maybe she could make him understand that it would be wrong to deny himself the chance of ever falling in love again.

And maybe she was using rose-tinted spectacles to view the situation because she was too cowardly to face the truth, a small voice whispered.

She ignored it with some difficulty, but she'd been telling the truth when she'd told Jack once that she was an optimist. How she prayed that she wasn't going to be proved a silly little fool!

'And you're quite sure that he's going to be all right?'

Yvonne couldn't hide her concern and Meg heard Jack sigh. Richard was in Recovery at that moment with Kate keeping a careful eye on him as he came round from the anaesthetic. Yvonne had been waiting for them when they'd left Theatre and it was obvious to Meg that she'd been crying.

'I can't make any promises as yet, Yvonne. However, I'm hopeful.' Jack's tone was gentle as he gave Yvonne a reassuring hug. 'We got the bullets out and that's the first step, so let's just take it a day at a time.'

'You're right. I know you are. It's just so hard…' Tears welled into Yvonne's eyes again and she turned away with a broken sob.

'I'll go with her,' Meg offered immediately.

'Would you?' Jack's gaze was intent when he looked at her. 'It's a difficult situation, isn't it? But, then, what relationship ever runs smoothly?'

She had no idea what he'd meant by that. However, there was no time to ask him as Alison came along the corridor just then to see how the surgery had gone. Meg quickly excused herself and hurried after Yvonne, closing the door as she followed the other woman into the waiting room-cum-lounge.

'Are you all right?' she asked solicitously, sitting down opposite her.

'Yes. No. Oh, I don't know!' Yvonne laughed shakily as she hunted a tissue from her pocket and blew her nose. 'I feel sort of up in the air, as though I don't know whether I'm on my head or my heels, if you know what I mean.'

'Only too well!' Meg heard the rueful note in her voice and quickly tried to pass it off. Yvonne certainly didn't want to hear her problems! 'I take it that you didn't expect to run into Richard again like this?'

'Not really, although I suppose the possibility was always at the back of my mind. Maybe that's why I offered to fly out here—who knows?'

Yvonne stood up and began pacing the floor. 'It's all such a mess! I don't know what to do and that's the worst thing. Now Richard might…might die, and I couldn't bear that!'

Meg got up and put a comforting arm around Yvonne's shoulders. 'You mustn't start thinking like that. The surgery went well so you must try to be positive.'

'I'll try.' Yvonne managed a watery smile. 'After all, he had two of the best surgeons in the business working on him, didn't he?'

'He did, indeed. Jack always does a brilliant job,' Meg agreed sincerely, unaware just how much her voice betrayed.

'You really admire Jack, don't you?' Yvonne's tone was thoughtful. 'Is it just his work you like or him as well?'

Meg shrugged, a little colour touching her cheeks at the rather too astute observation. 'Of course I like him. Jack's a great guy.'

She looked round as the door suddenly opened. Her colour deepened when Jack came into the room. His gaze lingered on her flushed face for a moment before he turned to Yvonne with a smile.

'Just thought you'd like to know that Richard is awake and asking for you.'

'Oh, I'll go and see him right away.' Yvonne hurried from the room and a small silence fell after she'd left.

Meg shifted uncomfortably. Was it her imagination or did the air seem to be full of a strange kind of tension?

It bothered her even though she wasn't sure as to its cause.

She hurried to break the silence at the same moment that Jack spoke. They both stopped then Jack shrugged.

'You first.'

'No, it wasn't anything important. What were you going to say?'

He looked momentarily uneasy, which surprised her and seemed to add to the overall feeling of tension. Her hands unconsciously clenched as she mentally prepared herself for what he might say.

'I just wanted to apologise, Meg,' he said simply. 'I was way out of order when I said what I did about you and Richard before.'

'Why did you say it?' Meg bit her lip, wishing that she'd simply accepted the apology with good grace. Did she really want to go into the whys and wherefores?

Jack took a deep breath and she knew that he was finding this incredibly difficult. His voice grated roughly when he answered. 'Because you were right.'

'Right? About what?' She stared at him in confusion, seeing myriad expressions chase across his face. There were so many that she felt dizzy from what she was witnessing, felt dizzier still when he actually answered her question. Frankly, it was the last thing she'd expected him to say!

'About me being jealous, of course!'

The admission was tinged with impatience, as though Jack resented having to disclose it. Meg licked her lips because they felt parched all of a sudden.

'W-were you?' She winced when she heard the wispy little voice she barely recognised as her own emerging from her lips. However, it was hard to behave as though this were an everyday occurrence.

Jack had just stated—quite clearly, too—that he'd been *jealous* at the thought of her being interested in Richard. This was definitely a red-letter day!

'Yes! I just said that I was.' Jack must have heard the bite in his voice, just as she'd heard it. He took another deep breath and stalked to the window, but it was impossible to see any thing with the steel shutter being locked into place so he couldn't fall back on that old ploy.

Meg felt her lips tilt with the beginnings of a smile and struggled to control it. It wouldn't be at all tactful to let Jack see that she was amused. After all, it must have cost him dearly to make that admission so it wouldn't be right to…to smile about it.

Her mouth curved a bit more and she clamped small white teeth around the edge of her lower lip to make it behave, but it was a losing battle. To hear Jack say that was the one thing in the world guaranteed to make her smile!

'What's so funny?' he demanded, looking round and catching sight of her expression.

'I…um…well, you know.' She shrugged, striving for nonchalance, although her heart was singing. Inside her breast there was a whole aria being sung, each swooping, soaring note lifting her spirits higher and higher. Jack had been *jealous*. It was like being handed a much-wanted gift!

'You think it's amusing that I should feel like that, do you?' He demanded, his brows lowering ominously. Meg smirked.

'I'll have you know it's never happened to me before and I sincerely hope that it never happens again either!'

Oh, he was really getting himself into a tizzy now! How typical, though. Most strong, self-reliant men would feel the same way about making themselves appear the slightest bit vulnerable.

That thought sent a rush of tenderness through Meg's body. Her smile was equally tender as she treated him to it. 'I hope that it never happens to you again too, Jack.'

She took a shallow breath then hurried on before her courage deserted her. 'There's no need to feel jealous about me and Richard or me and any other man, for that matter.'

'No?' His eyes seemed to gleam like smooth grey satin as they traced her face in a look which made Meg's heart seem to swell. She loved him so much but could he tell that just by looking at her?

'No.' She willed him to understand, willed him to take what

she was offering him and rejoice in what it could mean for them both. The future suddenly spread before her—long days full of love and laughter, commitment and sharing as they grew old together. Maybe she was presuming too much but this wasn't the time to start having doubts. If she could convince Jack that the future was theirs for the taking then it could come true!

'I'm not like Briony was, Jack. We are two different people.'

There was a moment when he stared at her and his eyes seemed to be full of everything she could have wished for, before the shutters came down. Meg could hear the sound of them falling inside her head and nothing had ever sounded so final before, apart from the tone of Jack's voice, of course.

'No, you aren't like Briony. You're everything she isn't— warm, caring, tender, loving. You're everything a man could want, in fact.' He reached out and touched her cheek then let his hand drop to his side.

'I just wish I'd met you first, but wishing doesn't change things. I can't erase the past, Meg. I can't pretend it never happened. All I can do is learn from my mistakes and never put myself in the position of repeating them.'

Her heart seemed to wither inside her when she heard what he said. 'So you prefer to remain alone for the rest of your life rather than take a chance again?'

His face filled with pain as he heard the anguish in her voice but his voice remained determined. 'That's right. I suppose it's the coward's way but it's far less painful at the end of the day, Meg, believe me. One thing I have learned is that there are no guarantees where love is concerned. It can end just like that and I'm simply not prepared to go through all that heartache if I can avoid it.'

He left the carriage without another word and Meg didn't try to stop him. She couldn't hold him against his will, couldn't make him take what she was offering if he didn't want it.

She took a deep breath.

She couldn't make Jack love her if he was no longer capable of loving.

'They were waiting in the trees…to ambush us…' Richard paused to gather his strength.

By tacit agreement everyone had gathered in the hospital bay after dinner that night. Richard had made a remarkable recovery from his surgery. Meg guessed that his rapid improvement owed much to the fact that Yvonne was sitting beside him, holding his hand as though she had no intention of ever letting it go again! It was obvious that they'd worked through their problems and reached an understanding.

Now Richard smiled as Yvonne held a glass to his lips so that he could take a sip of water. Meg looked away, finding it too painful to witness the look that passed between them. It just seemed to highlight how empty her own life was going to be now that Jack had turned his back on the possibility of them having a future together.

Unwillingly her gaze went to him and she coloured when she discovered that he was watching her. She turned away at once, not wanting to examine what had been in his eyes. What was the point in looking for something that wasn't there and could never be there?

She focused on what Richard was saying instead, but she was so conscious of Jack that when he shifted slightly she flinched as though he'd touched her. It struck her then that it was going to be impossible to stay on board the train in the present situation and that she would have to find some way of leaving.

'My men managed to fight them off and I don't think we shall have any further trouble from them.' Richard smiled thinly as he looked around. 'However, I intend to make sure that you aren't put at risk in any way. You will have an armed guard to accompany you for the rest of your journey.'

'If you really think it's necessary.' Jack sighed when Richard nodded. Obviously, he wasn't keen on the idea but was wise enough to accept the inevitable. 'Well, you know best, I suppose.'

He looked at the others. 'How do you all feel, by the way? Are you prepared to carry on as planned? If anyone wants to back out, just say so.'

There was a chorus of denials. Richard smiled. 'Thank you. I am sure that I speak for everyone in Oncamba when I say how much we appreciate what you are doing for us.'

The party broke up shortly after that. Richard needed to rest and everyone was tired from the stresses the day had brought. Yvonne followed Meg to the door, pausing to blow Richard a kiss, which he returned. She sighed as they walked along the corridor together.

'What happened today has to be the worst moment of my life. I hope I never have to go through anything like that again!'

Meg smiled sympathetically. 'It must have been scary for you. It was bad enough for the rest of us because we've all grown fond of Richard. I take it that you two have managed to sort things out between you?'

'Yes. It's just a shame that it took something as dire as this to make us both see sense.' Yvonne's tone was rueful. 'Richard and I have known one another for ten years now. We met at a ball one year when we were at university and were inseparable from then on.'

They had reached one of the exit doors and they both paused to look out. Smoke was rising from the village fires, pale grey tendrils spiralling into the cloudless sky. Night had fallen and everywhere looked so peaceful that it was hard to believe what had happened earlier in the day.

Meg leant against the carriage wall, feeling the heat from the sun-warmed metal against her bare arm. 'So what went wrong?'

'Life. Other people interfering. Doubts.' Yvonne shrugged. 'I knew I loved Richard and that he loved me, but I wasn't sure we could make our relationship work when the odds were stacked against us. Oh, it wasn't just racial prejudice, although we did encounter a bit of that. However, I think we were both scared of doing the wrong thing and that's what stopped us from doing what we wanted to do.'

'Which is?' Meg queried.

'Getting married and building a future together.' Yvonne suddenly grinned. 'However, nothing is going to get in our way now, believe me!'

She sobered abruptly. 'I just wish I could stay here and look after him. I can't bear the thought of flying back to England and leaving him here while he needs me so much.'

Meg straightened slowly. Her heart was heavy but she knew what she had to do. It was something she must do for her own sake but, more importantly, she knew that it would help Jack.

'There might be a way round that, Yvonne. How would you feel if I offered to swop places with you?' She smiled tightly when the other woman looked at her in surprise. 'You're desperate to stay here and I am desperate to leave so it would make sense, wouldn't it?'

'This has to do with Jack, hasn't it?' Yvonne asked quietly. She sighed when Meg nodded. 'Being in love isn't easy, is it? But are you sure this is the best way to handle the situation, Meg? I know from experience that running away doesn't solve the problem.'

'I know that. But I know that it's best if I leave, best for me and for Jack.' Meg took a deep breath because it was so hard to say the words out loud. 'Jack doesn't love me, you see. Having me here is just an embarrassment for him. It would be easier for both of us if I went back to England.'

'I'm still not sure that you're doing the right thing but if it's what you want, then, yes, Meg. I'll gladly swop places with you.' Yvonne reached out and hugged her. 'But that doesn't mean I've not got my fingers crossed that you two can work things out!'

'I wouldn't hold out too many hopes, Yvonne. Some things just aren't meant to be, and this is one of them.'

They parted company after that. Yvonne slipped back into the hospital bay to tell Richard the good news that she would be staying while Meg went to find Jack. The sooner she sorted this out the better it would be.

He was in his compartment when she tracked him down. He didn't say anything as he opened the door wide so that she could enter. Closing the door, he turned to look at her and it was impossible to gauge what he was thinking from his expression so Meg didn't bother trying. There was no point looking for things that weren't there, hoping for something that would never happen. It was time to face the facts and deal with them.

'I've just been speaking to Yvonne,' she began without any preamble. 'I've offered to swop with her and fly back to England with Bill and Katu so that she can remain here with Richard. I thought I should clear it with you, although I can't see that it will cause any problems.'

'If that's what you want to do, then it's fine by me.' Jack's tone was flat. 'Yvonne is well used to this sort of work so it won't cause any problems.'

'Then that's all that matters, isn't it? Good!'

Meg heard the overly bright note in her voice and hurried to the door before her control gave way. She reached for the handle then paused when Jack spoke softly behind her.

'I appreciate everything you've done while you've been with us, Meg. You've been a valued member of this team.'

Her heart felt as though it was going to shrivel up and die when she heard the impersonal note in his voice. Was that all she'd really been to him—a valued member of his team?

She didn't say anything as she opened the door because she didn't trust herself not to say something she might regret. She went to her compartment and packed her belongings then got ready for bed, but sleep was impossible. Tomorrow she would be leaving and the thought of not seeing Jack again made her feel as though the light had gone out of her world.

CHAPTER ELEVEN

'I JUST heard you were back! What happened? I thought you were due to stay in Oncamba for three months?'

'I was.' Meg smiled as Maggie Carr came rushing into the office to find her. Maggie had been on holiday since Meg had returned to work at Dalverston General two weeks previously. It was Maggie's first day back and she was on a late shift. However, it was obvious that she was dying of curiosity so Meg launched into the story she'd told so many times in the past weeks that she was word perfect. Nevertheless, she mentally crossed her fingers, hoping that Maggie would believe all the half-truths.

'So it ended up with me flying back to England to accompany the two patients who needed treatment.'

'How come you had to do it?' Maggie frowned. It was obvious that she'd sensed something wasn't quite right with the tale. 'I take it the patients were being flown back by air ambulance, so why wasn't a nurse sent out to bring them home? That's the normal procedure in a situation like that.'

'She was, only she wanted to stay in Oncamba.' Meg quickly explained about Yvonne wanting to remain behind with Richard. 'I offered to swop with her. It seemed the most sensible solution in the circumstances.'

'I suppose so…' Maggie still wasn't wholly convinced and Meg inwardly sighed. She really didn't want to go into the whys and wherefores. It was too painful to recall how Jack had made no attempt to dissuade her when she'd told him she was leaving. Had he been glad that a nice tidy solution to his problems had been arrived at with so little upheaval? Probably!

Meg pushed back her chair, unable to sit there and talk

about what had happened. Her emotions were too raw to discuss it, even though she knew that Maggie would be sympathetic if she told her the truth.

'I'd better go for my lunch. I need to get a bit of shopping as I've nothing in the flat to eat. How did your holiday go, by the way?'

'Don't ask! I should have smelt a rat the minute Nonna rang and told me how much she wanted to see me!' Maggie's eyes flashed. It was obvious that something had upset her and Meg paused on her way to the door.

'I thought you said that your grandmother had been ill and that was why she wanted you to spend your holiday in Italy with her?'

'That's the story I was given.' Maggie sighed. 'However, it turned out to be a ploy to get me there so that Nonna could indulge in a little matchmaking. She looked as fit as a flea, I'll have you know!'

Meg chuckled. Maggie's family's frequent attempts to marry off their eldest daughter were a source of great amusement to her. 'So what was he like this time? Cross-eyed and geeky as usual?'

'No...' Maggie coloured when she saw Meg's astonishment. 'No, he didn't have cross eyes, neither was he geeky. Just the opposite, in fact. He was absolutely drop-dead gorgeous, if you want the truth.'

'Then what was the problem?' Meg demanded, astounded by her friend's attitude.

'The *problem* was that he had to be the most arrogant, egotistical, self-centred man I've ever met!' Maggie stated emphatically, glaring at her. 'Do you know what he had the gall to say to me, that he wasn't the marrying kind so it would be better if I didn't get any ideas in my head? I ask you, is that arrogant or what? Just because he's some top-notch surgeon over in the States, he seems to think he's God's gift to women!'

'Well, he certainly made an impression on you,' Meg observed pithily, watching the angry colour sweep up her friend's face.

'Oh, he did. And it was all *bad*! Still, the one consolation is that I'm highly unlikely to run into Luke Fabrizzi ever again!'

Maggie stormed out of the office and Meg sighed. It sounded like a disastrous holiday but at least talking about it had distracted her friend from asking any more awkward questions about Meg's early return to England. From her—admittedly selfish—viewpoint it could be seen as a blessing.

There really wasn't anything she needed from the shops because it had been just an excuse to get away. However, Meg decided to go into town anyway. She'd found, increasingly, that she became restless if she didn't keep busy and that her mind started to wander along paths she preferred to avoid if it had nothing to occupy it.

She left the hospital and headed along the road. The day was grey and overcast, a heavy layer of cloud blotting out the sun and settling like a pall over the bustling market town. Meg wandered along the high street, thinking how odd it felt to be back in Dalverston, even though she had been home for two weeks now. She'd grown used to the space and freedom of Oncamba, become accustomed to waking each morning to a cloudless blue sky. Funny how easily you got used to something and grew to love it…

Her mind veered away from that thought because she was afraid where it would lead. However, it was less easy to stop herself thinking back over what had happened since her return to England. She'd spent the first three days in London, getting Katu settled in the hospital where she was to be treated. She'd also visited Bill, who was having to undergo a series of tests to check that the parasitic infection had been successfully cleared up.

Once Meg had been sure that they were both being well cared for, she'd returned home to Dalverston. She'd been intending to have a short break to recuperate but her flat had seemed so empty that she hadn't been able to bear it.

She'd rung Roger Hopkins, the hospital manager, and told him that she would like to come into work. He'd been only too happy to agree. Getting back into the busy hospital routine had been a relief, something positive to focus on, but Meg knew that the pain was just being held at bay. Not allowing herself to think about Jack, it made life bearable but it didn't change things. She loved him and missed him, and would have given anything in the world to have him love her in return. Nothing could compensate for the fact that it would never happen.

The church clock struck the quarter-hour and she realised that it was time to start heading back. Meg quickened her pace, not wanting to be late and delay another member of staff from going for her lunch. She turned in through the hospital's gates then stepped onto the grass verge as a car turned in after her. She glanced at it as it passed and felt her heart ricochet around her ribs when she caught sight of the driver.

Jack!

Meg's mouth worked but no sound came out. Not that she had any idea what she wanted to say. Seeing Jack here, it seemed to have stolen her ability even to think, let alone voice her feelings!

She took a quick breath, hoping it would calm her. It didn't work. Her heart was still playing ping-pong with her ribs, her nerves fizzing with tension. It took her all her time to walk up the path, and she ground to a halt when she saw that the car had stopped outside the main entrance and that Jack had got out and was waiting for her.

A great surge of emotion welled up inside her when she saw him standing there. Her legs were actually trembling as she forced herself to walk the last few yards. His face didn't alter as he watched her walking towards him; it held the same grave expression that she'd seen on it so many times in the past that it left her feeling more confused than ever.

Why had he come? What did he want? The questions were uttered silently inside her own head because she didn't have the strength or the nerve to ask them out loud.

'Hello, Meg. How are you?'

'Fine. And you?'

'Fine.'

As an example of sparkling repartee it wouldn't have won any awards, but Meg's heart rejoiced. Just hearing his voice again, that was so wonderful that she found it difficult to disguise her feelings.

She chose a point beyond Jack's right shoulder and stared at it, rather than allow herself to look at him. She knew it was better to avoid doing that because she simply couldn't be responsible for her actions. How would Jack feel if she launched herself into his arms and kissed him? She had no intention of finding out!

'Look, Meg, we need to talk,' he suddenly bit out with a touch of asperity. 'Is there some place we can go?'

He looked round impatiently, drawing her attention to the fact that they were attracting a great deal of interest. There were staff coming and going, with it being lunchtime, and a lot of inquisitive eyes were focused on them. However, Meg knew that it wasn't just the fact that they were standing slap-bang in the middle of the entrance which had aroused so much interest. Jack was so good-looking that he was bound to attract a great deal of attention wherever he went from the female of the species!

The thought annoyed her, although she knew that she had no right to feel that way. 'I'm afraid that's impossible. I'm due back from lunch in...' she checked her watch '...two minutes precisely.'

Jack uttered something harsh under his breath. 'Then we'll have to meet later. What time do you finish?'

'Five. But what do we need to meet for? What is there to say?' She squared her shoulders, struggling to keep the pain from her voice. 'I know the score, Jack. So what point is there in rehashing over old ground?'

His eyes narrowed when he heard the challenge in her tone. He took a slow step toward her and his eyes glittered dangerously as they centred on her face. 'Because I haven't flown seven thousand miles to stand here in full view of everyone and swop pleasantries!'

'It would be a first if you had—said something pleasant, I mean,' she shot back.

'You could be right. I don't seem to have a lot of luck when I open my mouth and try talking to you, do I, Meg?' He treated her to a decidedly wolfish smile as his hands fastened on her shoulders. Before Meg knew what was happening she was in his arms. 'Still, they say that actions speak louder than words, don't they?'

The kiss was hot and full of passion. And it was over almost as fast as it had begun. However, Meg's head was reeling so much that it took her a second to appreciate that fact.

Jack laughed softly and the sound held more than a hint of satisfaction. 'I'll see you at five o'clock, then, darling. Don't be late.'

He got back into his car and drove away. Meg blinked. She felt as though she'd just been woken up in the middle of a dream. Had that *really* happened? Had Jack been here and…and kissed her?

She touched her mouth with the tip of her right index finger and shivered when she felt the heat that still lingered there from that kiss. It hadn't been a dream at all. It had actually happened. Now all she had to work out was why it had happened and what it could mean.

Her heart began bouncing around again. Maybe it was silly to feel as though her birthday and Christmas had both come together but it was hard not to. Surely—*surely*—Jack wasn't the kind of man to kiss and run?

Jack was waiting outside the main doors when Meg left work at precisely two minutes past five that evening. She'd broken all records getting changed out of her uniform into her street clothes so consequently was rather out of breath. Seeing him standing there robbed her of what little bit of air she had left

'Hi,' he said softly, taking hold of her hands and pulling

her towards him. He kissed her lightly on the mouth then stepped back with obvious reluctance.

Meg struggled to draw in a tiny whiff of air but it was simply too difficult to perform that everyday function. Whether it was the kiss or the fact that Jack was there, she couldn't seem to make her body obey her. She saw him frown and heard the growing uncertainty that crept into his voice when she remained silent.

'Maybe I'm being too presumptuous, Meg. After all, why should you be pleased to see me after the way I've behaved?'

Why, indeed? Apart from the fact that she loved him to death and had longed for this moment, even though she'd never dared hope that it would happen!

Meg could hear the answer inside her own head but no words came out. Maybe it was the lack of oxygen that was causing the hold-up because there didn't seem any way she could force them from her lips.

Jack's eyes clouded with pain when she still didn't say anything. He turned to stare along the path and she saw a nervous tic start in his jaw as he struggled to retain control of himself. 'I shouldn't have come here, obviously. I'm sorry. I was wrong to put you on the spot like this.'

He swung round and began striding rapidly down the path. Meg stared after him in disbelief. Was he *really* walking out on her? Was she *really* going to let him? With an almost superhuman effort she managed to force some air into her lungs then used it to expel some sound at last.

'Jack, wait, damn you!'

Well, maybe that wasn't *quite* what she'd been intending to say, but it did the trick. Jack stopped dead in his tracks, although he didn't turn round. Meg muttered grimly under her breath as she stalked down the path after him. What would it have cost him to look round and maybe smile, even quirk a brow if smiling was beyond him?

She'd whipped herself up into a real snit by the time she reached him, but all it took was a glimpse of his expression to make it disappear. Jack was upset and hurt and as mixed up as she was. Just seeing the evidence of it on his face made her *ache* to put her arms around him and hold him tight, tell him that there was no need to worry…

She did it anyway. She slid her arms around his waist and held him, feeling the resistance in his body instantly melt. His arms came around her and he held her to him, as though he were trying to draw her deep inside himself, held her as though he would never let her go again.

'I love you…'

'I love you…'

They both spoke together then stopped and tried again. Meg laughed because she simply couldn't contain her joy at that moment.

'We sound like an echo!'

'Or two people who are meant to be together.' Jack cupped her chin as he looked deep into her eyes, and what she saw in his was everything she could have wished for. 'I love you, Meg Andrews. I've flown seven thousand miles to tell you that so I hope it sounds as good to you as it does to me.'

'It sounds great!' Meg blinked back her tears, laughing at her own foolishness. 'I don't know why I'm crying. Maybe it's because I'm so happy and can't believe this is really happening. I think you should pinch me so that I'll know I'm awake!'

'Oh, I know a much better way than that…' Jack's lips were tender and loving when they closed over hers. They said words he hadn't said, made promises he would make later. It was a sort of Morse code without the blips and the bleeps, and Meg's joyful heart had no trouble deciphering the message.

Jack drew back and smiled at her, his gaze both rueful and adoring. 'I think we should get out of here, don't you?'

He glanced pointedly over her shoulder and only then did she realise that there were at least a dozen cars lined up in the driveway, waiting to get past them. Her cheeks were flushed as she and Jack stepped onto the verge while the cars drove past. There was a lot of tooting of horns, not to mention some pithy comments from several of Meg's colleagues shouted through the car windows.

Jack shook his head in mock dismay as he took hold of her hand and led her to where he'd parked his car. 'I think I'll have to marry you now. I'll have the whole hospital after me for besmirching your honour if I don't!'

Meg treated him to a haughty look but her heart was thumping as she took in what he'd said. 'I hope you have reasons for wanting to marry me other than saving my honor. Not that you've asked me yet, and neither have I agreed!'

'Oh, I have, I have!' Jack backed her up against the car, trapping her between the solid metal and his own equally solid body. 'Want me to show you what they are?'

He kissed her slowly and thoroughly, letting the weight of his body rest against hers so that she was left in little doubt about his feelings. Meg was once again having problems with her breathing when he raised his head but the one consolation was that Jack seemed to be having just as much trouble with his.

'Yes, I'd love you to show me,' she managed to squeak. 'But not here! We don't want to shock everyone, do we?'

'A woman who speaks a lot of sense. I'll add that to the plus column, Meg, although it's getting a little overcrowded now.' He unlocked the car then dropped a kiss on the tip of her small, straight nose. 'The minus column is totally empty, however.'

Meg laughed as she slid into the seat. 'I can't believe that, Jack Trent! Surely I must have the odd fault? I'm only human after all.'

'Nope! I tried to find faults, believe me, but it was a waste of time and effort because I couldn't come up with a single one.'

He walked round the car and got in then turned to face her. Cupping her cheek with his hand, he looked deep into her eyes. 'I love you, Meg. I love who and what you are. I love the way you care about your work and about the people you work with. I love the way you'll fight for something you want or believe in. I love your stubbornness and determination as well as your tenderness and compassion. There are no minuses. They are all pluses.'

'Oh, Jack!' She turned her head, pressing a kiss into his palm, feeling her heart overflowing. It didn't seem fair that anyone could feel as happy as she felt at that moment. It was more than anyone deserved.

'I love you so much,' she whispered.

'I know. And to think I was almost fool enough to lose you, too.' A spasm of pain contorted his face before he summoned a smile, but Meg realised that if she'd found the past few weeks difficult to bear then Jack had found them no easier. It simply made her love him even more, if that were possible. That Jack didn't try to hide his vulnerability from her made her see how great a trust he'd placed in her.

'However, I've seen the error of my ways and I'm not going to be such an idiot again. Now, where to? I think we need some place quiet where we won't be disturbed. There's a lot we need to talk about.'

Meg smiled at him, loving him with her eyes as she would love him with her body very soon. 'Only talk, Jack? Oh, I think we'll find other things to do as well as talking.'

'Damn, this bed is cramped.' Jack groaned as he eased onto his side. Meg laughed as she traced the bridge of his nose with a gentle finger.

'I haven't had much use for a bigger bed, I'm afraid.'

'Then I'm not really complaining.'

He drew her into his arms and kissed her with a hungry urgency which quite belied the fact that they'd just spent the past couple of hours making love. Despite Jack's avowals that they would talk, they'd said very little since they'd arrived at Meg's flat. She'd opened the door, let them in and that had been that. Their hunger for each other had been just too great for them to wait, but now it was time to clear up any small misunderstandings, she realised without the slightest hint of misgiving. She loved Jack and he loved her. Nothing else mattered when put into that context.

'Right, you said that we should talk so maybe now is the right time.' She snuggled into his side, letting her hand rest on his muscular chest. She felt his muscles flicker and bunch, felt the response which affected other parts of his body. A wave of heat washed through her and she shifted languorously and heard him groan.

'I won't be able to think straight, let alone form a coherent sentence, if you do that!' He fastened a hand around the curve of her hip and held her still, although she was pleased to note that it didn't make all that much difference. His body was deliciously responsive to the nearness of hers...

She hid her smile, savouring the sweetness of that thought. 'Sorry.'

'Mmm, I bet you are. Witch!' He kissed her quickly. 'I knew you were going to be trouble from the minute I clapped eyes on you, Staff Nurse Andrews! I was right, too.'

'Why? What did I do?' She paused but the question had to be asked, even though she no longer feared the answer. She just didn't want it to upset Jack. 'Was it because I look like Briony?'

'No.' He must have felt the start she gave because he grinned at her. 'I can honestly say that it never crossed my mind that you looked at all like Briony. Maybe there is a slight resemblance in the fact that you're both blonde and beautiful but that's all. I never compared you to her. I just compared the *reaction* you had on me.'

Meg drew herself up and looked at him. 'What do you mean by that?'

'The only other time I'd been so instantly attracted to a woman, as I was to you, was when I met Briony. But I soon realised that you were far more dangerous because it wasn't just your very beautiful face and body I liked but your mind as well.'

He sighed as he ran a gentle finger down her cheek. 'Briony a very shallow person—she's only interested in anything that directly affects her. You are very different, Meg. You care so much about other people and that was apparent even at your interview. It scared the socks off me, I don't mind admitting, because I realised that if I'd been hurt by what Briony had done then it could be so much worse if I allowed myself to feel anything for you. It was a risk I swore I wouldn't take.'

Meg could barely keep her voice level. 'You…you mean that you thought you could come to love me more than you'd loved Briony?'

He must have heard the faint quaver because his smile was so tender that it brought a lump to her throat. 'No. I mean that I *do* love you more than I ever loved Briony. It wasn't long before I realised that I'd fallen head over heels in love with you, which was why I was so…well, difficult!'

'Difficult is an understatement! I never knew if I was on my head or my heels, Jack. One minute you were biting my head off for some misdemeanour or other and the next—'

'I was making it blatantly obvious that I had other things on my mind apart from taking you to task!' He sighed ruefully. 'I behaved abominably. I know that. My only excuse is that I was fighting for my sanity, or so I believed. I kept telling myself that you couldn't possibly be as wonderful as my own eyes were telling me you were, which is why I was so hard on you.'

'And you knew from the time of my interview that I was going to be a problem?' she asked smugly.

'Oh, yes. Not that I admitted it to myself, mind you. Certainly not! That would have been far too easy.' He laughed deeply, his warm breath stirring her hair as he drew her back into his arms. 'If I gave you a hard time, darling, I gave myself an even harder one, believe me!'

'Good! You deserve to have suffered for what you put me through. Not that there weren't some good times, mind.' She pressed her mouth to his chest and gently bit him, smiling when she heard the swift indrawn breath he took. 'Like the time we found Katu and sat outside the hut…'

'And when you came back on board the train after the other

went to the village to celebrate that wedding.' Jack's tone was husky. 'I didn't know whether to curse Miriam or drop to my knees and thank her when she interrupted us that night, because if she hadn't we would have made love.'

'And that wasn't what you wanted?' she teased, secure in the knowledge that he loved her. It felt wonderful to know that after all the uncertainty.

'Oh, I wanted it.' He bent and kissed her hungrily. 'I wanted it more than I've ever wanted anything in my whole life. But I knew that it would be wrong.'

'Wrong? How could it have been wrong, Jack?' she demanded, frowning at him.

He kissed away the frown lines which puckered her brow. 'Because I wasn't prepared to admit to you or myself how deeply in love with you I was. It would have been wrong to make love to you and then tell you that there was no future for us, and at that stage I was sure that there *wouldn't* be a future for us. I was trying to do the honourable thing, believe it or not, Meg!'

He tried to make a joke out of it but Meg knew that it was the truth. Jack had wanted her but hadn't wanted to hurt her by seeming to take what she would have given so willingly and then throw it back in her face. It was just another indication of how much he cared, not that she needed it. Just being here like this, loving him and having him love her back, that was all the proof she needed!

'I appreciate that, well, I do now. I didn't back then!' She kissed him tenderly then drew back and smiled at him. 'What made you decide to forgo the Sir Galahad act and come to find me?'

'Oh, several things. Richard for starters.' He smiled ruefully. 'I've been like a bear with a sore head since you left. You ask anyone and they'll tell you that. When you suggested swopping with Yvonne and returning to England, I thought it would be for the best. However, thinking and feeling are two very different things, I soon found out!'

Meg laughed. 'You deserved to suffer! I went through agonies remembering how you didn't try to dissuade me from taking Yvonne's place.'

'I'm sorry, darling. I never meant to hurt you.' He kissed her gently. 'You have to understand that I was so mixed up that I barely knew what I was doing most of the time. I messed up badly but I swear I'll make it up to you, if you'll let me.'

'Oh, I can be magnanimous if the situation calls for it,' she assured him. 'Anyway, what was it Richard said to make you see sense?'

'That he hoped it wasn't going to take a bullet to make me see what I was in danger of losing.' Jack sighed as he smoothed her hair with a decidedly unsteady hand.

'It started to put everything into perspective. Then I heard from the agency that they were thinking of sending you to India—they're instigating a project there to try to eradicate TB, which is a huge problem in the country. I realised that if you were sent there it could be months before I saw you again

'I'd already asked to extend my stay in Oncamba. I think at the back of my mind I'd been hoping that you would be asked to return as well but, obviously, that wasn't going to happen. It hit me then that my life was going to be meaning less without you as a part of it. I wanted you with me all the time, not thousands of miles away in a different continent! realised that Richard was right and that I had to do something immediately.'

'Remind me to give Richard a big kiss next time I see him! she declared. 'But now that everything is straight at last, where do we go from here? You mentioned something about marriage…?'

'I did. I haven't forgotten either.' He whipped back the sheet and climbed out of bed, going straight down on one knee.

'If I do this correctly, as all the books advocate, maybe I' get the answer I want. Will you marry me, Meg?'

She giggled. 'I'm sure Emily Post wouldn't have advocated a prospective bridegroom being naked when he made his pro posal! But let's not be picky about the details. Yes, Jack. I'll marry you, but on one condition.'

He scowled. 'And that is?'

'That you never try to leave me behind when you go off on one of your aid trips. To me marriage means being together no matter how difficult the circumstances are. It means sharing our lives, the bad bits as well as the good. I don't intend to be a stay-at-home wife while you go off to the jungle, playing Tarzan!'

'And I have no intention of letting you!'

He stood up, drawing her up so that he could kiss her. 'I accept your conditions. From what I recall, Tarzan found his soul mate when he found Jane. I've found you, Meg. You are my soul mate, the woman I love, the woman I want to spend the rest of my life with. Whatever life brings from now on, we face it together. And that reminds me—I forgot to mention I have to fly back to Oncamba tomorrow.'

'Tomorrow?' Meg stared at him.

'Uh-huh.' His grin was wicked. 'When I contacted the agency and told them I had to fly back home because there was something that needed my urgent attention, I promised that I would be away no longer than three days. I knew that would be all the time I'd need, you see. I'd either be able to persuade you that you couldn't live without me or you'd tell me to get lost.'

He kissed her again, letting her know how little appeal that last idea had held. 'However, it does mean that I'm due to be on a plane in...' he checked his watch '...just over ten hours' time.'

'Correction—*we* shall be on a plane in ten hours' time.' Meg kissed him quickly, then drew him down into her welcoming arms. 'Let's not waste another second, then. We've said everything that needs to be said, don't you agree, Jack?'

'Oh, I do. I most certainly do...!'

MILLS & BOON®

Makes any time special™

Mills & Boon publish 29 new titles every month. Select from...

Modern Romance™   Tender Romance™

Sensual Romance™

Medical Romance™   Historical Romance™

MA

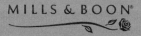

FREE

4 BOOKS
AND A SURPRISE GIFT!

We would like to take this opportunity to thank you for reading this Mills & Boon® book by offering you the chance to take FOUR more specially selected titles from the Medical Romance™ series absolutely FREE! We're also making this offer to introduce you to the benefits of the Reader Service™—

- ★ FREE home delivery
- ★ FREE monthly Newsletter
- ★ FREE gifts and competitions
- ★ Exclusive Reader Service discounts
- ★ Books available before they're in the shops

Accepting these FREE books and gift places you under no obligation to buy; you may cancel at any time, even after receiving your free shipment. Simply complete your details below and return the entire page to the address below. **You don't even need a stamp!**

YES! Please send me 4 free Medical Romance books and a surprise gift. I understand that unless you hear from me, I will receive 6 superb new titles every month for just £2.49 each, postage and packing free. I am under no obligation to purchase any books and may cancel my subscription at any time. The free books and gift will be mine to keep in any case.

MIZEC

Ms/Mrs/Miss/Mr ....Initials ....

BLOCK CAPITALS PLEASE

Surname ....

Address ....

....

....Postcode ....

Send this whole page to:
UK: FREEPOST CN81, Croydon, CR9 3WZ
EIRE: PO Box 4546, Kilcock, County Kildare (stamp required)

Offer valid in UK and Eire only and not available to current Reader Service subscribers to this series. We reserve the right to refuse an application and applicants must be aged 18 years or over. Only one application per household. Terms and prices subject to change without notice. Offer expires 30th September 2001. As a result of this application, you may receive further offers from Harlequin Mills & Boon Limited and other carefully selected companies. If you would prefer not to share in this opportunity please write to The Data Manager at the address above.

Mills & Boon® is a registered trademark owned by Harlequin Mills & Boon Limited.
Medical Romance™ is being used as a trademark.